A scandalous mar[riage to a]
roué—undertaken t[o pay his]
gambling debts—ha[s left her]
reputation ruined. W[hen she flees]
from the court of V[ersailles to]
Scotland, she finds that her name is a byword there as it
has been in France. James MacLeod believes the stories
and treats Isabel as he thinks she deserves, yet finds
himself falling in love with her: slowly, Isabel's frozen
heart melts again. Then James learns that she is meeting another man in secret, as if she were the wanton he
first thought her. . . .

Castle of
the Mist
Valentina Luellen

MILLS & BOON LIMITED
London · Sydney · Toronto

First published in Great Britain 1972 by
Robert Hale Limited, Clerkenwell House,
Clerkenwell Green, London EC1R 0HT

This edition published 1981 by
Mills & Boon Limited, 15–16 Brook's Mews,
London W1A 1DR

© Valentina Luellen 1972
Australian copyright 1981
Philippine copyright 1981

ISBN 0 263 73433 1

Set in VIP Baskerville 11 pt Solid by Fakenham Press Limited

Made and printed in Great Britain by Cox & Wyman Ltd., Reading

To Roy with love—
For thirteen more

CHAPTER
ONE

'I wish you would take my advice and go to France for a while,' Isabel said, looking at her brother with anxious eyes. 'You would be safe there and I could stop worrying.'

Duncan MacLeod leaned over the chair where she sat and gently ruffled her blonde hair.

'For the last time, I'm not leaving you alone at Asher Mor. If you find out the truth you'll need help—Malcolm would kill you too, you know that.'

Isabel nodded, her thoughts dwelling for a fleeting moment on the dark caves which ran from beneath the house to the sea-shore, and she shivered at the memory of the cold water lapping around her waist. Even as a child Malcolm, her elder brother, had always been insanely jealous—and she had almost died because of it. She had not seen him in six years—not since her marriage had dragged her from the two people she loved most in the world—her father and gentle Duncan who stood at her side—the most hunted man in the Highlands—a branded murderer. Yet another victim of Malcolm's vindictiveness.

'Where will you go now?'

'Back to the mountains. I know the countryside and I have many friends. There are a dozen men with me now—and some women and children too. When Malcolm discovered they had given me help he drove them out of their homes—on two occasions he burned the crofts.'

'He hasn't changed,' Isabel said bitterly, rising to her feet.

'No—he hasn't, little sister. That's why I have my fears about you returning to the house.'

'It's my home. Oh, Duncan, you don't know how much I've longed to come back. To you—to father—to walk along the cliffs where we played as children. How did I bear it for so long?'

A frown creased Duncan's thick brows as he stared down into his sister's face. In six years she had grown from a lovely young girl into a beautiful woman. The dark blue travelling dress she wore, trimmed with an abundance of lace, brought a touch of Paris to the drab room in which they stood. Her long blonde hair swept back from her face was caught up with a dark-coloured ribbon tied in a bow, and fell in ringlets over her shoulders. The way she had always worn it before she was married, he remembered.

At first glance, he had thought she had changed very little, but as they had talked he noticed several differences. Her reluctance to discuss her marriage—or why she had chosen to remain a whole year in Paris after her husband had died, instead of returning home to those who loved her. And her eyes—those tawny eyes he had never known not to sparkle. He had not seem them register emotion of any kind since she had stepped off the boat in Scourie the previous day. When she smiled they remained dull. Whenever they talked—they became wary, almost suspicious.

He knew her life in France had often been miserable, but he was only now beginning to realise the effect it had had on her. Outside was beauty, but what was inside? he wondered. Bitterness—yes, that for certain, perhaps hatred too for the father who had sold a seventeen-year-old girl into marriage with a man of sixty. For Malcolm too—whose wild gambling fever had brought about the whole unhappy affair.

'Was it very bad?' he asked gently.

Isabel turned from the window and looked at him.

He saw the guarded expression had returned to her eyes. Would they never hold laughter again, he wondered?

'Yes—it was, but it's over now. Julian is dead and I am very rich. I intend to make up for all those lost years.'

'Is that why you stayed in Paris?'

'When you came to me in Versailles and asked for sanctuary, I gave it to you without asking any questions. What is it you are really asking, Duncan? "Are the rumours about me true", perhaps? You tell me you are no murderer, and I believe you because you are my brother and I love you. Have you so little faith in me?'

'Good God, Isabel! Could you ever believe I killed her? I loved the girl,' Duncan interrupted, growing pale.

'Do you believe me to be a whore?'

'No.' Duncan stepped forward and gripped her by the shoulders. 'Don't ever call yourself that again.'

'Others have—and will. Hold me, Duncan—let me feel your strength. As long as you believe me, no one else matters.' With a sigh Isabel laid her head against her brother's shoulder, comforted by the pressure of his arms about her. 'If only you had been with me these past years. . . .'

'The past is behind you,' Duncan murmured. 'With your looks—and money—you'll have every man for miles courting you.'

To his amazement Isabel tore herself out of his arms with something sounding suspiciously like a sob.

'You fool! Do you think I'm going to fall into the arms of the first man who comes along?'

'I didn't mean that. I meant the next time you marry, the man will be of your choice. Father has never forgiven himself—he won't stand in your way.'

'I have no intention of ever marrying again,' Isabel replied stiffly. Moving across to the bed she picked up her cloak and secured it around her shoulders with hands that shook visibly. Duncan crossed to her and stood looking at her in concern.

'What is it, little one? You've changed so.'

'Yes—I suppose I have. Don't ask me to talk about it now, Duncan—it's too—unpleasant.'

'Do you mean there is more than you've told me—more than Julian's unreasonable attitude over him not being able to give you a child?'

Julian's unreasonable attitude! Isabel thought—if only it had been that simple. During the first months of the marriage she had prayed she would not have the child of the husband who came as a stranger to her in the night with one purpose in mind. Little over a year later she was praying to be *enceinte*, and so free herself from his insane plans to beget an heir—plans which were to become more devious and hideous as the years passed—plans which were to fail and, in doing so, brand her as a whore. With a supreme effort she controlled the trembling which seized her every time she remembered those terrible times and looked into her brother's face.

'There is much I will tell you, but not now. First we have to prove your innocence. After that—we shall have all the time in the world to talk over past mistakes. Come in——' she turned as there came a knock on the door and waited for it to open.

Simone, Isabel's French maid, curtseyed from the doorway. Behind her stood her brother, Jean-Paul. Both had served Isabel since the first year of her marriage—their introduction into her household and their subsequent positions of trust caused many a raised eyebrow in the court of Versailles, for both came from the 'Beggars' Quarter' of Paris—the district which lay beyond the Pont-Neuf and was the playground of thieves, prostitutes, beggars, both real and false. No stranger was safe in the honeycomb of dark streets and

people disappeared without trace and without any
questions being asked.

Simone and Jean-Paul Ratan had run a tavern in one of
the more squalid side-streets, catering for clientele from
swarthy-skinned gypsies and cut-throats to bored
gentlemen of high birth who sought diversions other
than those provided by the 'Sun King' and his pavilion
entertainments.

A slight smile touched Isabel's mouth as she looked
at Simone in the new dress and the bright-coloured
cloak trimmed with fur she had bought for the journey.
She was a lady's maid to perfection. No less the gentle-
man in looks was Jean-Paul, but the appearance was a
deceptive one. Honest labour had not changed him one
iota, Isabel mused—he was still a product of the back
alleys. Danger and excitement were the food which had
filled his stomach when he was a mere boy, and he
longed for them still.

He possessed a dangerous temper and the cunning of
a hunted fox, yet no one would ever know it if they came
face to face with him. His dark features were expressionless as they looked first at her, then the man at her
side. Isabel had never been able to guess what thoughts
lay behind that inscrutable face, and at times it
annoyed her, but compared to the great service he had
rendered during her marriage it was a triviality she
could well overlook.

'What is it, Simone?' Isabel asked. 'I gave orders I
was not to be disturbed.'

As his sister hesitated, Jean-Paul took the initiative
and, stepping past her, he pointed to the window.

'Half a dozen riders have just arrived. One of them
asked for you by name, Madame.'

Isabel looked at Duncan in dismay. Had he been
seen? Were these soldiers come to capture him? Or
Malcolm's men? If the latter, he would never leave the

inn alive. Motioning him to stay back she crossed to the narrow window and stared down into the cobbled courtyard. There were at least six men. She knew none of them.

Her eyes alighted on a tall man crossing towards the doorway directly below her room. The plaid he wore was instantly recognisable as that of the clan MacLeod and there was something vaguely familiar about the hard-set features of the man himself as he briefly glanced upwards.

'James MacLeod!' Isabel gasped. 'Why is he looking for me?'

'Not you, my sweet,' Duncan muttered, his hand falling to the sword at his side. 'Over Kirsty's grave James vowed to hunt me down. More than once he's come within a hair's breadth of catching me. It's a shame—we were friends once.'

'Once I believed in fairy tales,' Isabel returned dryly. 'He can't know you are here. I'll head him off. Jean-Paul, you come with me just in case the MacLeod proves difficult.'

Duncan looked from his sister to the handsome Frenchman at her side and felt a shiver of apprehension run through him. The protective instinct he felt for Isabel told him that this man would kill to keep her from the slightest harm. Had Isabel's disastrous marriage changed her to the extent where she might contemplate using him as a weapon against those who had spoiled her youth—or against James MacLeod, if he had indeed come seeking the man accused of murdering his young ward?

Isabel turned back to him and her lips lightly brushed his cheek. Over her shoulders Duncan saw an almost imperceptible tightening of Jean-Paul's mouth. Good God, he's jealous, he thought in amazement. Was it true, then, the wild rumour he had heard in Paris that this servant was her lover? He said himself she had

changed—but how much? What was the unpleasantness she refused to speak of?

'Stay here. Jean-Paul and I will make sure he doesn't
come upstairs,' she whispered. 'Take care, Duncan.'

'I was about to give you the same warning. James is
no fool.'

Isabel gently disengaged herself from his restraining
grip.

'He's a man, isn't he? How can I contact you?'

Duncan's eyes flickered disdainfully across to the
man behind her.

'Your servant will always find me if he rides east from
Sandwood.' He used the word 'servant' in a deliberate
attempt to show his dislike of the liaison. Isabel did not
seem to notice his intention and turned away. Jean-
Paul hesitated a moment, then followed. The smile on
his face told Duncan that the gibe was considered unimportant.

'Watch over your mistress, girl,' Duncan ordered
Simone, who stopped to pick up Isabel's gloves before
leaving.

'Both Jean-Paul and I would lay down our lives for
her,' the woman replied sincerely. 'Do not worry,
monsieur, Madame la Marquise has learned to take
care of herself. She is a match for anyone.'

Even for Malcolm? Duncan wondered as he closed
and barred the door after her. Was anyone a match for
Malcolm?

At the bottom of the stairs Isabel came face to face with
James MacLeod, and at once found herself coming
under the scrutiny of a pair of pale green eyes which
swept her from head to toe. He was taller than she
remembered—and thinner. As children, Duncan and
Malcolm had been her only playmates, but often she
wandered alone through the great house at Asher Mor,
or sat in the kitchens listening to one of the older

clansmen relating tales of the great Viking galleys rounding Cape Wrath to raid along the coasts of Scotland, burning and killing and carrying off men and women as slaves. She loved her home—its desolation, its wildness; and the primitive savagery of her clan's history. The sight of the mist rolling back from the waters of the Atlantic and the sound of the waves breaking against the cliffs beneath her rooms. These things had been an important part of her childhood and the memory of them had helped her during the long years away from home.

She was back where she belonged. The thought brought new strength to her trembling legs. She returned his stare with equal candour before stepping past him as if he was invisible.

'Simone, have the landlord bring down my luggage. Are the horses ready, Jean-Paul? I am anxious to leave this dreary place.'

'Saddled and waiting, Madame——'

'Isabel MacLeod!' With a bow James MacLeod stepped between her and the outer door. 'Or should I address you as the Marquise de Riché? Do you not remember me?'

'Should I?'

A slight flush rose beneath the man's brown cheeks at her icy tone. He hesitated, unsure of himself, which was exactly what Isabel had intended.

'Your face is familiar,' she continued. 'Are you one of my father's men? Has he sent you to meet me?'

'I think you know me well enough. Think back now, who put you over his knee for breaking the leg of his favourite horse with your carelessness.'

'It was an accident, James MacLeod, and well you know it,' Isabel retorted indignantly. Then, as she saw the laughter on his face, her attitude softened and she acknowledged his victory. 'I remember you, though only just. I've been away a long time.'

So long that she had forgotten the only time she had ever been spanked by anyone other than her father. She remembered the incident now. She had been fourteen, grown out of childhood, but not yet a woman, and terribly vulnerable to Malcolm's warped sense of humour. He had been in a mean mood that day, made worse when she found him forcing himself on a frightened servant girl in one of the attic rooms. At nineteen, Malcolm drank to excess, gambled heavily and boasted to have a line of women from Asher Mor to Inverness. His violent moods were unpredictable and all the servants in the house were afraid of him—and so was Isabel. His threats and oaths had sent her rushing from the room, holding her head which rang from the cruel blows he had rained on it. Frightened out of her wits that he might follow, she had run out of the house and ridden away on the horse saddled in the courtyard.

Four hours later James MacLeod and her brothers had found her limping painfully homeward after the horse had stumbled and thrown her—breaking a leg in the process. The sound of Malcolm laughing was in her ears as James unceremoniously hauled her over the nearest rock and administered a sound spanking to an already bruised area before riding off to catch and destroy his horse—his favourite, she was to discover some time later.

'Your father asked me to meet the boat at Kinlochberie,' James said. 'I was presented with a pile of luggage, but no passengers. Were you ill?'

'No—bored. I thought it would be pleasant to go the rest of the way from here on horseback. Why did my father not come himself?'

'He's been ill these past six months, surely you knew,' James began, then he broke off with a grimace. 'Of course—I was forgetting you have had no communication with him since you went away. Don't you think it was rather harsh to send his letters back unopened?'

'Was it not harsh to marry a girl of seventeen to an old man to repay a debt?' Isabel demanded bitterly, stirred to retaliation by the unjustness of his words.

They also awakened her conscience. Once the first letter had been returned with a letter of her own stating she wanted no further communication with him, the die had been cast—even though she had regretted it throughout all the years she was away. Duncan's letters had kept her informed of what was going on—but although her father continued to write many letters she never once opened them.

'A debt of honour.' James stared at her grimly. He was not sure what he had expected, certainly not this dangerously attractive woman with the face of an angel. A somewhat tarnished angel, he thought from what he had been told, and he would not forget it. Nevertheless, she was still the loveliest creature he had ever encountered.

'I don't intend to stand here discussing affairs which are none of your business,' Isabel said, drawing on her gloves. 'As for escorting me, I prefer to ride by myself.'

'I did not make this extra journey to return to Asher Mor alone,' James said, with a sudden hardening of tone. 'I suggest you begin to show your father some of the respect lacking these past six years by doing as you are told without further argument. You are in the Highlands now, Madame, not Versailles. I won't ask you again—I'll have my men tie you on to a horse. And tell your servant that if he shows an inch of his blade I'll run him through.'

Isabel spun about in alarm at the threat and saw Jean-Paul's fingers curled around the hilt of his sword. She laid a gloved hand across his.

'No—he means it. In Scotland you will find most men still retain the barbaric instincts of their forefathers. They raid the lands of their enemies—burn and plunder the crofts and steal their cattle and make free with the unfortunate women. They need little or no excuse to provoke a fight. Remember it, and do not be goaded into drawing your weapon. Come now, show me my horse and let us go.'

James smiled, but said nothing as she picked up her skirts and swept past him into the courtyard. His eyes watched the Frenchman help her to mount the white-stockinged bay, held by one of his men, convinced they were lovers. Why else was she so anxious to avoid a confrontation?

Good God, what did it matter? he thought, stepping outside. If she was as easy as Malcolm had led him to believe, he could take her at his leisure.

Isabel could not leave without a farewell to Duncan. As she swung her horse about, her hand was raised briefly as if to smooth back her hair. Somehow she knew he was watching her from the window and had seen the gesture. Suddenly she did not even mind the infuriating presence of the Highlander riding beside her. James MacLeod would never know how close he had come to the man he had sworn to kill.

Familiar landmarks presented themselves as the journey progressed. The rounded heads of Ben Arkle and Ben Foinavon rose to welcome her and point the way home. James MacLeod rode in front of her with three of his men—the remainder brought up the rear behind Jean-Paul.

Looking into Simone's closed face, Isabel wondered what she thought of her new home. They had scarcely seen a dozen people since they left Scourie. Many of the crofts seemed deserted and the people they had seen had watched them pass by without a greeting or acknowledgement of any kind. The uprising of 1715 had taken place nine months after her marriage. Duncan's letters had told her both her brothers and her

father had come out in support of James Stuart. James
MacLeod and his father, too, had left their homes to
fight. She had lived those terrible months of fighting
with them and shed many bitter tears when the 'Pre-
tender' fled the country and returned to France. Behind
him he left many Highlanders who were to suffer great
hardship—privations and death because of their
loyalty.

Her father's glib tongue and a considerable amount
of money placed in the right hands had saved Asher
Mor, its people and their homes from destruction.
James MacLeod, who had lost his father in battle, had
returned home a bitter man, determined to fight to the
death to keep his home and lands from the English. It
had been Isabel's father who had tempered his anger,
and again persuaded the Government in London to
show leniency.

Isabel had never been able to understand the gesture
and had even resented it. The additional money which
had changed hands had reduced the House of Asher
Mor to poverty, and six years later it had barely recovered.

The mountains and lochs closed in behind them like
a protective barrier, and ahead the countryside was flat
and more desolate than any they had so far passed
through. Four hours of steady riding had brought them
to within two miles of Asher Mor. To the right of Isabel
were pockets of water trapped between the thick carpet
of heather and to her left the sea. She could hear the
crashing of the water against the base of the cliffs and
rode closer to the edge, exhilarated by the sound which
was music to her ears. A fresh Atlantic breeze caught at
her hair, blowing it about her face in wild disorder and
brought back memories of childhood days when she
had run wild like a tinker's child and revelled in her
freedom.

Her eyes bright with tears, she lifted her head to the

huge grey house outlined against a backcloth of blue sky, and a deep sigh escaped her lips.

'I could be wrong, but I think you are glad to be home,' James remarked. So engrossed was she in her own thoughts she had not heard him ride up. 'I hope you will not find it boring after the gaiety of Versailles?'

A pleasant reply died on her lips at his sarcasm. A woman of her reputation would not be expected to live a quiet existence, which was all she had to look forward to in this part of the Highlands. Was he offering a diversion—an *affaire*, perhaps?

'I am quite accustomed to providing my own entertainment,' she answered quietly, and without any outward sign of the anger his words aroused.

Foolishly, she had believed the life she had lived in France would end once she returned to Scottish soil, but of course Malcolm had anticipated that. A few well-placed words had made it impossible for her to become the same girl who had left Asher Mor. The mockery dancing in James' eyes left her in no doubt as to what he believed her to be, despite his courtesy and helpfulness throughout the journey. How long would it be before he—and others—grew tired of being polite?

She had no choice but to go on as before. This time there was no Duncan to take her part against Malcolm, but she was no longer afraid of her elder brother. He would not find her a girl easily reduced to tears but a woman brought to maturity by five unhappy years, and hardened by miseries only two other people had shared—Jean-Paul and Simone. She was a match for Malcolm and for men like James MacLeod, who looked at her with bold eyes and considered her an easy conquest.

'Would you like to rest a while?' James asked as she lingered to look out across the sea.

'No—I am anxious to be home. Has it changed much?'

James's face hardened visibly as he gazed at the desolation around them.

'Everything has changed since the war—the English saw to that. These last few years have not been easy for any of us. I know there were many times your father was on the point of writing you to come home, but pride forbade him to beg.'

And Julian, her husband, would never have allowed her to leave him, Isabel thought. She had only succeeded in doing so once and the nightmare of the days following her forced return would forever haunt her dreams.

'My family has always had more than its share of pride,' she replied, turning her horse about.

James pulled his mount in line with hers. His eyes were thoughtful as he asked, 'How much do you know of what happened here—concerning your brother, Duncan?'

Isabel had been waiting for such a question since they had left Scourie. She looked at him with slightly raised eyebrows, her expression betraying nothing.

'If you mean the death of your ward, why not say so? Duncan is far too gentle a man to commit murder.'

'Malcolm and his steward were witnesses.'

Isabel shrugged her slim shoulders.

'Then he has obviously changed. We were close once—as children, but circumstances or time can easily change people into strangers.'

'As it has you,' James remarked in a rough tone. 'I used to admire your closeness to Duncan—it often made me wish I had a sister. Now I'm glad I haven't. I hope to God he doesn't expect any help from you, because he won't get it, will he? You haven't cared for anyone but yourself for years, you selfish bitch.'

Isabel went white with anger, brought to the point of retaliation by his rudeness. Only with a great effort did she control herself. Her rôle demanded indifference to

Duncan and his plight. It was the only way she could get at the truth.

'In Versailles that is the first rule of survival,' she said. 'I have come home for a holiday, not to be involved in my family's petty squabbles.'

'I'm pleased to hear it,' came the stony reply. Spurring his horse ahead, he rejoined his clansmen, leaving Isabel to realise how near she had come to a heated argument with him.

Something about him put her instinctively on her guard, and it was nothing to do with Duncan. His arrogance, perhaps—or the way he looked at her. Somehow she knew it was neither. She had known many arrogant men and most of them had looked at her in the same distasteful way. They did not like her reputation, but it did not prevent them from wanting to take her to their beds. James MacLeod was acting no differently, and yet——?

She was allowing the strain of her homecoming to make her imagine things, Isabel thought, and dropped back to talk to Jean-Paul.

The fortified house at Asher Mor had been built in the fifteenth century by Donald MacLeod, last surviving member of the family who had been born and raised on the island of Skye—as had generations before—and who had died in one of the bloodiest phases of a long-lasting feud between the MacLeods and MacDonalds.

With a dozen clansmen Donald had come to the mainland and built a new house. He called it Asher Mor, after the place where the boats had landed. Here he had married and raised a family, venturing from behind the protection of the thick walls only to raid the lands of his enemies or to supervise another addition to the fortifications.

Generations of MacLeods had ensured no one, MacDonalds or any other clan, would massacre unsuspecting clansmen, their wives and children. Donald's great-grandson had a moat built around Asher Mor, draining water to fill it from a nearby loch, thus making the only access across a wooden bridge, wide enough for one rider at a time.

'Are you all right, Madame?' Simone rode close to her mistress, noticing how pale she had become as they reined in their horses in the inner courtyard.

Isabel quickly nodded as James MacLeod handed the reins of his horse to a clansman and came to help her dismount. A tremor ran through her body as he lifted her to the ground. She saw his mouth tighten as he mistook it for something else. She had not realised the sight of the old house would arouse such emotion. She felt like a child again—excited—eager to explore and to see familiar faces.

As she entered through the huge, double brass-hinged doors into the hallway, an old man came to meet her. There were tears in his eyes as he went down on one knee, and taking both her hands in his pressed them to his lips.

'Welcome home, Mistress Isabel. Do you remember me—Lachlan—your father's steward?'

'Lachlan—of course I do. I've only been away six years, it isn't a lifetime,' Isabel answered quietly. The greeting had touched her, for this man had been a close friend and confidant since her childhood, yet at the same time she sensed he was reproving her for cutting herself off from everyone.

He rose and stepped back, his eyes taking in the two people behind her at a single glance, then fastened on the expensive travelling gown Isabel wore and the diamond brooch fastened at her throat.

'You were a bonny lass when you went away, but you're a grand lady now. It will do the master good to feast his eyes on you. He was worried when you didn't arrive on time. Will you go upstairs to him now?'

Ruthlessly Isabel squashed the urge to do just that.

'In a while, Lachlan—the journey has tired me. I will take some refreshment in the *salon*. Is my brother expecting me?'

'He is waiting to receive you in the drawing-room. I will inform him you have arrived.'

Isabel did not miss the displeasure in Lachlan's eyes. He was thinking she had changed in more than looks.

'Do that, and please be good enough to find quarters for my servants—as near my apartments as possible.'

'The master has had your old apartments in the south wing made ready. They shall have the rooms at the end of the corridor.'

'Thank you, Lachlan. Perhaps you will show them the way,' Isabel said with a smile, and went into the *salon*.

The room had not altered. The warm afternoon sunshine streaming through the windows slanted across the portrait of the beautiful woman above the open fireplace. James, coming into the room behind Isabel, stopped short and gazed in silent appraisal of the two women.

Mother and daughter were alike in every detail. Both had hair the colour of pale gold and sculptured features hereditary in generations of the French aristocracy of which Suzanne de Bray was a descendant.

A faint smile touched Isabel's pale face as she stared up at the likeness. Her mother had died giving life to a daughter who had brought disgrace on her proud name. In France the family had refused to receive her and had never once acknowledged her presence at court, despite the fact they came into constant contact at balls and soirées and the king's hunting party, and at the crowded palace at Versailles it became impossible for her not to come face to face with at least one relative during the course of the day.

She soon learned to accept the rejection and go her own way, Jean-Paul and Simone being instrumental in helping her over the difficult period.

With a sigh she turned away, pulling off her cloak and gloves, and James was almost certain he had glimpsed tears glistening in her tawny eyes.

'Don't you think you are being too hard on your father? He's a sick old man. Come,' James stretched out a hand towards her with a friendly smile, 'let me take you to him.'

Isabel stared at him, resenting neither the authority in his tone or his interference in a purely personal matter. All she wanted at that moment was to make peace with her father. She had been alone too long—and he was in ill health. They had need of each other. Wordlessly she nodded.

A hand beneath her elbow, James escorted her out of the room and across the hall towards the stairs. They had not taken half a dozen steps when a man and a woman came out of a side room and Isabel came face to face with her hated brother, Malcolm.

His appearance had changed little, she thought, staring into the hard brown eyes whose scrutiny had many times reduced her to tears—perhaps the mouth was a little crueller, but that was all.

'Lachlan told me you had arrived,' Malcolm remarked. His gaze flickered to James and the hand still holding Isabel's arm. 'I see you two have become re-acquainted. You must stay to dinner, James, and talk over old times—I'm sure Isabel has much to tell us of her years abroad. She's grown up, hasn't she? No longer the little sister I used to play with.'

'For which I am exceedingly grateful,' Isabel replied coolly. She motioned to the quiet woman standing beside her brother. 'Are you going to introduce us?'

'My wife. Mary—my sister, Isabel. You two will be the best of friends, I'm sure, although Mary has the advantage of knowing more about you, Isabel, than you do of her.'

The colour rose in Mary MacLeod's cheeks and her eyes fell before the anger rising in Isabel's face. Muttering the excuse that she had to instruct the servants for the meal that evening, she hurried away.

'I see you have found someone else to provide you with amusement while I was away,' Isabel said. Mary looked older than she was, but it was obvious that she was completely dominated by Malcolm and his twisted mind—as she herself had been as a child.

'She was Father's choice, not mine,' Malcolm declared with a careless shrug of his shoulders. 'You know how stubborn he can be when he makes up his mind. She's a shy little thing; having another woman around the house will be good for her. She lacks so many things—most of which France seems to have taught you. You are staying for some while, I suppose.'

'I have made no plans.' Isabel glanced up the stairs towards her father's room. 'A great deal will depend on how Father receives me.'

'Is that all! Then you are home for good—he hasn't stopped talking about you since the letter arrived to say you were coming. Even your apartments have been redecorated, though where the money came from I've no idea. We've little enough for essentials as it is. You've been returned to favour, Isabel—all sins have been forgiven. Father may be sick in his body, but not his mind. Your money will come in useful to put some order back into this house—what else but the thought of all that wealth could have induced him to have you back?'

'You seem to be labouring under a misapprehension, Malcolm.'

Isabel's expression was faintly amused and she saw the sudden hardening of the lines around her brother's mouth. He had expected her to be afraid of him—that their relationship would be on the same footing as before. Now was as good a time as any to show him she had no intention of allowing him to rule her as he did his unfortunate wife.

'I have been in France for six years, during which time I have become both a bride and a widow, inherited a great deal of money, two town houses and a château in the country. I have my own apartment at Versailles and a place in society which demands that I remain at court for most of the year. After a while that kind of life can grow quite tedious. I simply wanted a change. No doubt I shall find Asher Mor annoyingly quiet after a while, and then I shall go back to where I belong. And now, if you will excuse me, I am going to see Father.' She nodded briefly to James, picked up her skirts and went upstairs.

'The cool bitch. My God, she's been well taught.' To James's amazement Malcolm began to chuckle. He was annoyed at being a witness to the antagonism between Isabel and her brother. He was a frequent visitor to the house and he and Malcolm were on amiable terms, yet he had found himself disliking the way he had deliberately tried to provoke her, and he said as much. Malcolm looked at him through narrowed eyes.

'She took no time at all to win you over to her side.'

'I don't give a damn about her one way or the other,' James retorted. 'It's Alistair I care about—the two of you for ever at each other's throats isn't exactly an inducement for him to get well.'

'Are you telling me you don't find her attractive?' Malcolm demanded with a sneer. 'You have an eye for pretty women, James.'

'I'm not blind, I can see how beautiful she is, and if she's all you say—I know what could happen. That, I think, gives me a slight advantage. I just didn't like the way you tried to lead her into an argument the minute she was in the house again. Forget what happened. Give her a chance, Malcolm, for your father's sake.'

'You're a fool, James. She doesn't need any aid from you. By now she'll have Father eating out of her hand —tomorrow it will be Mary and all the servants. A pity Duncan isn't here to play her champion, too—he was rather good at it when we were children. By the way, did she say anything about him?'

'No—not really—she seemed only interested in her own welfare. I think she's a thoroughly spoilt young woman accustomed to lavish living and the attentions of too many men.'

'Why be so polite? She's a whore and I'll damned well treat her like one. I told you quite a bit about her, James, but I also left a great deal out—for the sake of the family, you understand, but as you seem taken with her it's best you know all there is. Come and have a drink, and I'll tell you how my sweet-faced little sister entertained a lover while her husband lay dying in his room.'

Isabel pushed open the door of her father's bedroom and quietly stepped inside. She had knocked twice, but received no answer. The windows of the room overlooked the cliffs and a sandy beach, two miles long. She could hear the cry of seagulls wheeling above the house and felt a fresh breeze on her face as she approached the silent figure in the chair by the open window.

'Father!'

The man turned slowly—painfully—his head inclined towards her. She was shocked at the change in him. At fifty-four Alistair MacLeod looked nearer seventy. The dark hair Malcolm had inherited was completely white, the thick-set features ravaged with pain. The brown eyes stared at her, yet did not appear to see her.

'Suzanne—is that you?'

Suzanne—her mother! Isabel felt the tears start to her eyes. Was he so ill he did not recognise her?

'No, father—it's Isabel.'

She watched his lips move soundlessly, feeling her composure gradually slipping. The war had begun all this, he had never really recovered from a bad chest wound, but she knew she, too, was to blame. All those letters returned unopened—total withdrawal on her part from the father who had needed her desperately.

How could she have been so blind, so selfish—he had done no more than any father would have, given the same circumstances. He had had no way of knowing the life she was to lead—the misery she would have to endure at the hands of the man to whom he had entrusted her safe keeping. He would have to know—she had to vindicate herself in the eyes of the most important person in her life.

'Isabel——' her father's voice shook with emotion. When she did not move he tried to rise from his chair, but the effort proved too much and he fell back with a groan.

'Why do you stand there and stare at me as if I am a stranger? Haven't I suffered enough? Malcolm rules my house as if I am already dead. Duncan is a hunted murderer. We live in poverty from the war and the clan scarcely survives from day to day. Am I for ever to see your reproachful face before me, too? Forgive me——!'

It was a pitiful cry from the heart of an old man too sick to be proud. Blinded by tears, Isabel threw herself into the trembling arms outstretched towards her.

'Father—oh, Father! I've come home.'

CHAPTER
TWO

ISABEL lay outstretched on the huge four-poster bed watching her maid unpacking the last of the trunks which had accompanied her from France. She had slept soundly for over three hours, awakening refreshed and with renewed strength to face Malcolm again.

Her rooms had been very pleasantly decorated, she thought, looking around her, and all the furniture and silver ornaments were as she remembered them. Nothing had been changed. Lachlan had told her how her father had locked the rooms after her departure and allowed no one, apart from himself, to enter. Her meeting with him had drained her of all anger and resentment and left her with an empty, ashamed feeling which had followed her into the realms of sleep. Questions had been impossible—they could come later, she thought, sitting up. Now the breach had been closed, it would be easier for them both.

'What do you think of my home, Simone?'

'It is very grand, Madame, but——' the maid broke off with a shrug of her shoulders. 'I cannot understand why you left the château to come to this place where every hand is turned against you.'

'Not every one,' Isabel murmured with a smile. 'I have made peace with my father.'

'You have told him the truth?'

'Not yet. He is my father and I love him despite everything. I didn't realise how much until I saw him again today. Explanations can come later—if necessary.'

'Your brother will make sure they are.' Simone

continued to put away Isabel's dresses in the long wall closet. 'That one hates you, and the other, the one you call the MacLeod, he is little better. You should have stayed in Versailles—better the devil you know.'

'Don't worry about me, Simone, I am no longer a child. I am not afraid of Malcolm—and what harm can he do me? I must stay and try to help Duncan.'

'And where was he when you needed him?' Simone asked dryly.

'That is not important. He needs me now and I intend to do all in my power to prove him innocent of the murder of James's ward.'

Isabel got up and crossed to the window. It overlooked the cliffs and the sound of the sea was forever present in the room. She had forgotten how lovely the sound was. Tonight she would lie in bed and listen to it and it would be as if she had never gone away. She watched Simone lay out her dress for dinner that evening and a determined look crept into her eyes.

'No—I won't wear the blue. Put out the white satin and my diamond necklace.' The latter was Duncan's wedding present. Perhaps it would provoke Malcolm to comment and so allow her to begin probing into the mysterious death of Kirsty Fraser. 'Do you want to go back to France?'

Simone looked up at her mistress in open-mouthed surprise.

'And leave you here alone? *Mon Dieu*—why do you ask? Do you want me to go away?'

'Oh, no, Simone,' Isabel answered, 'but I owe you and Jean-Paul so much already. I have no right to ask you to stay here and perhaps risk your lives. If Malcolm did kill Kirsty he will not be above killing again to hide the fact, and I think it would give him great pleasure to do away with me. He tried once when I was a little girl—didn't I tell you?'

Simone's pale features became even paler. 'Indeed

you did not. I thought we had no secrets from each other.'

'This happened many years ago—and it is something I wanted to forget. It is the only thing I have never told you.'

Isabel turned to look out of the window again. The sea roared in her ears and she was transported down to the tiny cave below the house. 'As children Duncan and I were inseparable. We had more in common with each other than with Malcolm and he resented the fact. He used to devise all kinds of methods to break up our games. Once we tried to teach him a lesson and neither of us would hold conversation with him for three whole days—he paid us back by almost drowning me.

'There is a cave below the house—many a night when I was a child I used to see ships anchored offshore and hear the smugglers unloading the wine casks into it. At high tide it is completely flooded. Malcolm tricked me into going in there and then barred the door leading back into the house. My escape by the beach was cut off by the tide. The water was waist-high before Duncan and Lachlan found me.'

'You told your father, of course.'

'And risk Malcolm's anger again? No—I never told him. Duncan guessed, and there was a terrible fight which he lost. He was far too gentle to be a fighter—or a murderer. Malcolm has much to account for. I only thought it fair to tell you the kind of man he is.'

'A man of violence.' Simone spread a beautiful white dress out over a chair, selecting matching accessories with loving care. 'If he so much as looks at you the wrong way I will push him off the cliffs or slit his throat while he sleeps.'

Isabel showed no sign of surprise at such an alarming statement. Simone was more an elder sister, wise in the ways of the world—an expert when it came to men—than a maid. Whenever they were alone, their relationship was a friendly one, never that of mistress and servant. Simone rarely spoke of her past, more out of respect for Isabel's innocence than fear of reproach for the kind of life she had led.

Motioning to the young woman to sit down, she loosened her long blonde hair and began to brush it. There were times when she missed her old life, but her concern for Isabel's welfare was greater than the longing to return to it.

She gave an annoyed frown as there came a soft tap on the bedroom door and Mary MacLeod came in.

Isabel turned with a smile.

'Come in, Mary. I was hoping you would visit me.'

'I don't want to disturb you. I was wondering if you will be dining with us tonight? Malcolm thought you might want to retire early.'

'On my first evening at home—nonsense!' She watched the woman slowly advance into the room, saw her eyes take in the open closet full of some of Isabel's magnificent ball gowns and day dresses, the jewellery laid out on the dressing table and the exquisite dress on the bed. A look of envy crossed her face, changing to one of surprise as Isabel said softly:

'Do you like my clothes?'

Mary looked down at the green satin dress she wore. It was two years old and the best in her wardrobe. She hoped the frayed lace on the sleeves did not show. With Asher Mor in such poverty there was little money for costly material, and it was more than her life was worth to ask Malcolm to give up some of his gambling money to buy a new dress for his wife.

'They are very lovely.'

'Simone, show Mary the burgundy velvet—with her colouring it should suit her very well. What's wrong?' Isabel asked as two fierce spots of colour burned on the other's cheeks.

'I don't want your charity.'

'I don't give charity.' Isabel motioned to the dress her maid held. 'It's yours if you want it, and you are welcome to have anything else which takes your fancy. In return I want you to tell me about Malcolm and Kirsty Fraser.'

'Malcolm is my husband and Kirsty was my best friend,' Mary answered coldly. 'I have no desire to talk about either. Why are you interested anyway? You care nothing for Malcolm. Duncan was always your favourite.'

'It's true we were close,' Isabel said, stepping into the gown Simone was holding, 'but I have been away for six years and a great deal appears to have happened during that time. Malcolm has probably told you I've had no contact with my family since my marriage.'

Mary nodded. Her eyes strayed to the burgundy dress hanging outside the closet. It looked as if it would fit her perfectly, and the colour was one of her favourites. What harm was there in retelling something that had already been common talk for over a year? Isabel was Malcolm's sister, after all—not a stranger.

'There is not much to tell. When James MacLeod returned home after the 'Fifteen he had made a promise to look after the daughter of a friend killed in battle. She came to live with him some months later. We became friends. Malcolm met her by accident—we were out riding at the time. Within six weeks James had given his consent for their marriage. They were very much in love.'

Isabel turned away to fasten a jewelled comb into her hair and her eyes were hard. Malcolm in love! He had never cared for anyone but himself—love was beyond him.

'And where does Duncan come into all this?'

'He began to press his attentions on Kirsty even at the betrothal ball. He refused to listen to her pleas to be left alone, and eventually he and Malcolm came to blows. Everyone thought it had brought him to his senses, but a few days before the wedding itself he tried to force her to go away with him. Malcolm and his steward heard her screams, but before they could reach them Duncan killed her.'

'How?'

'He strangled her—before their eyes. Malcolm managed to wound him, but he escaped and hid in the hills. I pray to God he will be caught soon so that my husband can have peace of mind again.'

Isabel turned on her curiously.

'Are you saying he is still in love with Kirsty? He is married to you.'

'The match was arranged by your father—he dearly longs for a grandson. With you gone—and Duncan, too——' Mary broke off, looking embarrassed. 'A man of Malcolm's wild ways doesn't fall in love easily. I shall never take Kirsty's place and I know it.'

'You must make a place of your own in his heart—never try to take the place of another,' Isabel murmured. Crossing to Mary's side, she kissed her on both cheeks and it was a spontaneous gesture of genuine affection. She both liked and felt sorry for her. Life in the shadow of Kirsty Fraser could not be easy. 'I would like us to be friends, Mary.'

'Sometimes it is difficult for two women beneath the same roof to get on together,' Mary said in a low tone.

'There is no reason for us to quarrel. Take me as I am and remember that this is my home, too—my family. It would be nice to be Isabel MacLeod again and forget the Marquise de Riché ever existed. You can make it easier for me.'

'I don't trust her.' Simone stared after Mary's departing figure with suspicious eyes. 'If she believes that tale her husband told her, she'll believe anything—and that doesn't leave you in a very strong position.'

'I like her.' Isabel fastened a diamond bracelet around her slender wrist and stood back to inspect her reflection in the mirror. 'Malcolm can be very persuasive at times, and she has no reason to disbelieve him.'

'Are you going to tell her the truth?'

'That Duncan fell in love with Kirsty after her betrothal to Malcolm and wanted to marry her himself? What proof can I give her—or that it was Malcolm who murdered her when he found her trying to run away with Duncan? I must bide my time, Simone, and we must both keep our ears and eyes open.'

'And what if Monsieur Duncan is caught before you have chance to find out anything?'

'Pray for it not to happen, because if it does I may have to ask for Jean-Paul's help.'

'He will give it gladly.'

'He has already killed twice for me, Simone—it must not happen again. I shall not need you again tonight, you may do as you please. By the way, where *is* Jean-Paul?'

'The last time I saw him he was making the acquaintance of a very pretty kitchen maid,' Simone replied smilingly. 'By tomorrow you should have all the latest gossip.'

So Jean-Paul was chasing the women already, Isabel thought amusedly as she made her way to her father's room. Still, there should be sufficient around to keep him happy during his stay. He was a man who always liked to have a woman somewhere in the background, and she had grown accustomed to the way he used and discarded them in the most amiable fashion. Yet during all the years in her service, he had never made one improper advance to her, despite the fact he had killed two men on separate occasions—one for insulting her, the other for trying to seduce her in the gardens of Versailles.

The servant had become a bodyguard and reputed to be her lover. He had laughed when he had first heard the gossip, but she remembered that the expression in his eyes had been far from amused, and at that moment she had known that Jean-Paul loved her. The realisation had worried her almost to the point of distraction, but as the weeks slipped into months and he continued to serve her with the same meticulous care, she knew he would never proclaim his feelings, and it would not be right for her to confess that she had found out.

Lachlan opened the door for her. His eyes appraised her appearance and with a smile he stood back for her to enter.

'You have done what all the doctors failed to do,' he said in a low tone. 'You have given him the will to live again. Bless you, mistress.'

Isabel could scarcely conceal her surprise at the man who stepped forward to greet her. Her father wore his best plaid and his grey hair had been carefully combed back into a queue and tied with a ribbon. With a bow which brought a grimace of pain to his face that she pretended not to notice, he kissed her on both cheeks.

'It was a poor welcome I gave you earlier. Welcome home, my child.'

'Father—should you be up?' Isabel asked slowly. It was a marvellous gesture on his part and it touched her deeply, but in his weak state she feared such sudden exertion might prove too much for his failing heart.

'Tonight we shall all dine together—our first family gathering in six years. You don't know how much I've looked forward to the day you came home.'

'You seem very sure I would.'

'Why not—this is your home. You belong here with your own kin who can protect you.'

'From what, Father, some amorous Highlander

who has heard of the Marquise de Riché? If I need protection, which is most unlikely, Jean-Paul will provide it.'

Alistair MacLeod's gaze roved over the exquisitely dressed figure before him. He could scarcely believe she was a widow with five years of marriage behind her—she looked no different from the day she went away—and yet she was. He sensed hidden strength behind the woman's frame and saw a hardness in her eyes which troubled him.

'Ah, yes—the man who came with you. Lachlan tells me he has the devil's own arrogance about him for a servant.'

'He is one of the few men in this world I trust implicitly,' Isabel said softly. She linked her arm through her father's with a smile that told him nothing, and he refrained from asking whether or not the man was also her lover, as Malcolm had suggested.

Malcolm and James stood together drinking beside the huge open fireplace as Isabel and Alistair came into the room.

'You see,' Malcolm sneered quietly, 'I told you she would have him eating out of her hand again. Look at the way she fawns over him—a pity she didn't spend a little more time tending her poor husband.'

James said nothing. All afternoon the only topic of conversation from Malcolm had been the scandalous conduct of his sister. She looked innocent, but she was not, he thought, taking his place at the table beside her. She looked beautiful, but that was only what men saw when they looked at her—beneath the surface was ugliness. And yet, as he repeatedly glanced her way during dinner, he realised it was not merely curiosity he felt about her. There was an attraction—he had felt it the first time he saw her again at the inn at Scourie. The wilful child had grown into a cold, calculating woman with an insatiable appetite for lovers whom she discarded with the same indifference she took them—if he was to believe all he had been told, and he had no reason to think that Malcolm should have lied about his sister.

He watched Alistair lean towards Isabel and say something to her and heard her soft laughter in reply. She was as close to her father as if she had never been away—or was it only a pretence? Where was the resentment she had spoken of—the desire to be revenged for six years of exile? If she hurt the old man in any way she would answer to him. He was as close to Alistair as if he had been his own father.

'We've scarcely heard a word from you since Julian died,' Malcolm said, looking across at her. 'It's almost a year now. What have you been doing with yourself for so long?'

'Enjoying the freedom you took away from me,' Isabel replied, smiling at him over the rim of her wine glass.

Malcolm threw back his head and roared with laughter.

'So it's true what we have heard about your insatiable appetite, my dear. Is it true no male is safe when you are about? No wonder poor Julian's heart gave out.'

Isabel's smile did not waver beneath her brother's insulting remarks, but James saw Mary look away in embarrassment and even Alistair's ruddy cheeks had grown pale. Was it only he who saw the murderous hatred blazing out of those lovely eyes—directed at the man who lounged opposite and dared to brand her as a whore beneath her own roof?

'There are other ways to be amused, such as losing money at the gambling tables,' she returned calmly, and James marvelled at her self-control. 'How is your luck these days, brother? Better, I trust—you have

nothing to barter with if you have a run of bad
luck—except your wife, of course.'

'That's enough out of both of you.' Alistair's fist hit
the table so hard the wine glass at his elbow tipped over,
staining the snow-white cloth the colour of blood. It
was an omen, Isabel thought, a moment of panic seiz-
ing her—the stain spread between her father, Malcolm
and herself. There would be blood between
them—Duncan's perhaps—or her own!

'Are you deaf, girl?' Alistair thundered in her ear.
Lost in her own thoughts, she had not heard him
demand an apology for her rudeness to Mary. 'I said
apologise or go to your room.'

Isabel's eyes held her father's. This is how he had
been years ago—the ruler of his own home and his
family. She had respected him then——

'No harm was meant,' Mary began, but Isabel interrupted her with a shake of her head, saying:

'My father is right, my rudeness was unforgivable.
No insult was meant to you, Mary, and my brother's
hide is too thick to have been touched by what I said.
Please accept my apology. The fact that Malcolm
used me to keep himself out of the Bastille is not your
fault.'

'My dear girl, I did you a favour,' Malcolm chuckled,
ignoring the warning look directed at him by his father.
'A rich widow at only twenty-three. Think of the years
ahead of you—you'll have suitors flooding to Asher
Mor by the score. Another husband is probably just
what you need—a little younger this time, eh?'

'I didn't come back to get married again.'

'Then why did you?' Malcolm's voice was suddenly
hard. His eyes narrowed with suspicion and as he
looked at her Isabel knew he did not trust her. She
shrugged her slim shoulders.

'I've told you once already—I was bored.'

'Is that the only reason?'

'If you mean have I come back because of Duncan, why not ask me?'

'Because his name is forbidden in this house.' It was Alistair who spoke. The mention of his youngest son had brought an unhealthy sallowness to his cheeks, and James silently cursed the thoughtlessness of his children. They were so intent on hurting each other that they could not see their quarrelling could very well kill their father.

Malcolm did not even take his eyes from Isabel's face.

'Well?'

'Don't bring me into your quarrel with Duncan—settle it with him, if you can catch him. And now, Mary, I think we will leave the men to their cigars and adjourn to the drawing-room. We can continue our earlier conversation.'

Isabel filled two glasses with wine and took one across to where Mary sat watching her.

'I want us to be friends, but I haven't started off on a very good foot have I? I really didn't mean to be rude.'

'I understand—at least I think I do. You and Malcolm hate each other, don't you?'

Isabel slowly sipped her wine. It was one of the bottles she had brought with her from her own vineyards. If she closed her eyes she could almost imagine herself back in the sprawling château. It was a long while before she answered.

'It's been this way since we were children. Sometimes I think he arranged my marriage to Julian because he hates me. No doubt he's told you his own version of what happened.'

'I'm only his wife,' Mary said with a shrug of her shoulders. 'Until a few months ago he rarely mentioned you—then when he heard of your husband's death he seemed to change. He became moody—and very short-tempered. When he learned you were to come home he was in a black rage for days. I thought he would have been pleased to see you.'

'Not now the positions are reversed.' Isabel looked around her with a soft sigh. 'So much has changed in this house—I've noticed many of Father's pictures have disappeared, his tapestries and his jade collection is down to one solitary little piece. I suppose he had to sell it all after the war. Times are difficult, and Malcolm has never liked being poor. When he ran out of gambling money he sold my jewels and when they didn't raise enough to keep him out of the Bastille, he sold me. He knew Julian was after a wife—a young wife to give him sons. I was married to him for breeding purposes only—and in return for services rendered, Malcolm's debts were cancelled.'

'But you never had a child,' Mary said quietly.

'A week after Malcolm and I came home, Julian arrived to ask Father for my hand. He agreed of course. We were married within a month under this very roof. I spent part of my honeymoon on board the boat taking us back to France. By the time I reached my new home I was praying for a child so that I would be left alone—but there was no baby. Julian blamed my coldness—he vowed to have a son no matter what it cost him.' Isabel drained her glass with a sudden shudder. 'It cost him his life—and me? He would be well pleased to see what misery he brought me.'

'You are rich now—and still young.'

'Young enough to take another husband as Malcolm suggested,' Isabel answered with a soft laugh. 'Oh, no, Mary. After five years I am once more alive and free, and I intend to keep my freedom. I have paid for it a thousand times over.'

'And emerged remarkably unscathed from your harrowing experience.'

Isabel turned slowly towards the door, veiling the

contempt in her eyes as she stared at her brother.
Ignoring him, she stepped forward to help her father,
leaning heavily on the arm of James MacLeod. He
looked exhausted, she thought, slipping a cushion
behind his back as he sank into the nearest chair.

'What have you two been talking about?' Malcolm
demanded as his wife rose to pour drinks for the men.

'Isabel has been telling me of France,' Mary replied
quietly.

'The latest court scandals, I suppose,' Malcolm
sneered, with a sidelong glance at his sister. 'You'll be
wanting to go there next.'

'Why not? It sounds interesting—and exciting.'

'You will be most welcome to stay with me at Versailles,' Isabel said, sitting down on the arm of her
father's chair. 'I can guarantee you won't be bored.
Disillusioned, perhaps. After a while you will find the
charming court ladies who flock to talk to a new arrival
are only interested in you as a source of new gossip, and
the elegant men who pay you compliments by the dozen
are terrible bores and worse whoremongers than any
men in Scotland.'

'Perhaps you have yet to meet a real man,' James
interposed, deliberately stepping forward to take his
glass from Mary so that he could watch the reaction
which sprang to her tawny eyes.

The flicker of a smile touched her mouth as she
glanced up into his face—a contemptuous twist of those
full lips that made him want to grab hold of her and
carry her upstairs and show her she had met such a
man.

'My brother deprived me of the chance to find a man
in Scotland before. Rest assured I shall seek one out if I
get bored.'

'If he is a real man he will do the seeking, Madame la
Marquise, and you will have no say in the matter.'

For the first time that evening a flush stole into

Isabel's pale cheeks. Not even Malcolm had achieved that victory, and he knew he had touched a vital spot. She needed the firm hand of a man she could not control with her beauty—or money—or womanly tears. A man accustomed to taking what he wanted—like James MacLeod.

Early next morning, scarcely before the mists had rolled back from the Atlantic, Isabel arrived in the stables to select a suitable horse for herself. She was running an experienced eye over the line of fine-looking animals when Jean-Paul appeared, and immediately confirmed her choice of the white-stockinged mare she had ridden from Scourie. For himself he picked a piebald stallion and ordered the stable-boy hovering in the background to saddle both.

'If Madame has no objections, I would like to ride with her.'

'I should like that. I had no idea you were such an early riser, Jean-Paul. Are your quarters not comfortable?'

'Perfectly.' A faint smile touched the Frenchman's handsome features as he helped her to mount. 'But since we arrived I've had little chance to appreciate it.'

'Her name is Maura, isn't it?' Isabel enquired amusedly.

'Simone's ears are as sharp as her eyes,' Jean-Paul replied, 'but you did tell me to make myself at home. The girl is *amusante*—and a chatterbox. She prefers talking to making love.'

'Was it time well spent?'

Swinging himself into the saddle, Jean-Paul cantered alongside her. They rode away from Asher Mor, along the cliff road towards the tiny village of Sheigra. Isabel looked expectantly at her companion.

'The girl's story differed little from the one we have

been told,' Jean-Paul answered at length. 'All the servants believe Kirsty Fraser was murdered by your brother, Duncan.'

'What am I to do, Jean-Paul? My father is a closed book on the subject, and I'm sure Malcolm is having me watched. His steward followed me everywhere yesterday. He is supposed to have witnessed what happened. I was tempted to approach him, but once I do that Malcolm will know my true reason for coming home.'

'That leaves only one person—James MacLeod.'

Isabel reined in her horse. When he helped her to dismount Jean-Paul felt her trembling and his eyes narrowed questioningly.

'Why does this man upset you?'

'Don't question me, Jean-Paul,' she returned abruptly, and walked away. He followed her down the narrow sandy path to the beach and across the golden sand to the water's edge. Isabel glanced back along the curving line of cliffs behind them. A mile or so away a peninsula of land jutted out into the water. On it stood a castle—its battlements obscured in mist.

'De'n Ceo,' Isabel said quietly. 'It means 'of the mist'. You can see how it got the name. I've only been there once. I was ten, I think, and I went to James's eighteenth birthday with my family and disgraced myself by being violently ill after a glass of wine. The day after Malcolm told me he had doctored it with whisky.'

'As unpleasant a child as he is a man,' Jean-Paul muttered.

'And dangerous—never forget that. Tell me what the talk is about James MacLeod. Is he really as close to my father as he pretends?'

'Since the death of his own father, yes. In that respect he seems genuine enough. Maura thinks he has—or had—a mistress in Durness, but says he's never shown any inclination to marry. His sole interest is his home and land.'

'Malcolm lost no time in telling him of my unfavourable reputation.'

'And how did he react?'

'Like a man—how else?' Isabel replied bitterly. 'He thinks me an easy conquest.'

'Then I shall have to disillusion him.'

Turning her back on De'n Ceo, Isabel walked slowly along the beach, stopping every few yards to pick a seashell out of the still wet sand. As a child she had often played here in Sandwood Bay, despite its reputation of being haunted. The debris from wrecked ships buried in the sand fascinated her. She and Duncan had played hide and seek among the rotting hulks and laughed at the tales of ghosts.

'No, Jean-Paul, I want no trouble between you and James MacLeod.'

Jean-Paul's face hardened visibly as he looked out over the water.

'Of course not, Madame, I understand.'

'No, you don't. I don't give a hang for James Mac-Leod, but I do know you wouldn't stand a chance against him in a fight, even with your cunning. Six years ago he was the best swordsman in this part of the country. I have no reason to think his prowess has diminished. I am being selfish and thinking of myself, Jean-Paul. If anything happened to you, what would I do? You must know how much I have come to rely on you.'

'I am sure Madame would have no trouble finding another servant from among her own household,' the Frenchman said, still not looking at her, but Isabel heard a definite softening in his tone.

'Are you not more than a servant?' she asked quietly. 'Are you not my friend, too?'

Jean-Paul swung around and she saw her words had

disturbed his indifferent pose. His eyes gleamed as he
stepped towards her, and for a moment she thought he
was about to reveal the deep feelings he had suppressed
for so long, but all he did was to take both her hands in
his and press them to his lips.

'I have grown so used to playing protector, I suspect
every man who looks at you. It must be the devil in me.
Forgive my possessiveness, Madame, it will not happen
again.

'Come—help me back up the path, I want to show
you more of our beautiful Scottish countryside,' Isabel
returned lightly. She was inwardly relieved that Jean-
Paul had once more contained himself. He was the last
person she wanted to hurt with a rebuff.

His fingers curled tightly around hers as he helped
her over the rough pathway to where the horses were
tethered. With effortless ease he lifted her into the
saddle and sprang on to his own horse. Isabel found her
hands were shaking as they gathered up the reins. For a
strange, frightening moment it was James MacLeod
who held her, not Jean-Paul—his face hovering inches
from hers, arrogant, mocking.

During the ride homewards, Isabel deliberately rode
close to Craeg Riabhach, where her brother and the
loyal men who followed him were hidden. From the
heights of the mountain she knew he must be able to see
her. It was her way of letting him know he was not
forgotten. It was a great temptation to urge her horse
up the slopes and make contact, but somehow she
restrained the impulse. To be seen in the vicinity by
Malcolm or any of his men might arouse suspicion. To
be caught on the mountain itself would confirm the real
purpose of her return to Asher Mor.

Jean-Paul's expression was sympathetic as she
turned the mare back towards the cliffs.

'Be patient, Madame, you have only been home two

days. When the excitement of your return is over, perhaps the talk may flow more easily. I am certain the servants have been warned to watch their tongues. It took me a full night to get young Maura to even mention your brother Malcolm's name. They fear him as much as the devil himself.'

'Sometimes it is hard to distinguish between the two,' Isabel said. Her eyes lingered on the hawklike profile of the man at her side. She would never understand him. He loved her, yet he never spoke of how he felt and never once had he attempted to take advantage of the girl he had chosen to serve. For this reason above all others, she trusted him more than any man. 'I want you to take the first ship back to France, Jean-Paul.'

'Madame?' He looked at her as if she had taken leave of her senses.

'You will remove the furniture from the house in Paris and put the place up for sale. My father could use the money badly, and I never want to go there again.'

It was the house where Isabel had spent the long weeks of her honeymoon. Every room, especially the bedroom on the first floor where she had been abused and humiliated, served as a reminder of her husband. After his death she had had it closed and gone to live at Versailles, spending occasional weekends at the château near the beautiful Forest of Bray, attended by only Jean-Paul and Simone and a small household of servants who had been with her since her marriage.

'Have the furniture brought to Asher Mor—it will bring the old house alive again. While you are away I am going to visit friends in Inverness. By the time I return the excitement of my homecoming may have died down, as you say, and we can get on with the task which brought me back.'

'The Countess of Sevigné was always interested in the Paris house. If she is still interested I may be able to effect a sale before I return.'

'Do whatever you wish,' Isabel said with a smile. 'I know I can confidently leave the matter in your hands. Just hurry back as quickly as possible.'

'Madame, we have company,' Jean-Paul muttered, staring over his shoulder towards Sandwood Bay.

Isabel's eyes fastened on the riders fast approaching them. Had Malcolm followed her—or sent men to watch her? With the exception of one man the green and blue colours in their plaids identified them as MacLeods. She stiffened as one of the riders reined in, then wheeled in their direction, motioning his companions to follow suit. She needed only one glance at the darkly tanned face beneath the bonnet with the eagle's feather of a chief to know they had been found, not by her brother, but by the one man she wanted most to avoid.

CHAPTER
THREE

'SHALL we ride on, Madame?' Jean-Paul was alarmed by the pallor which was creeping into Isabel's cheeks. She looked almost afraid as she gazed at the approaching riders. His eyes narrowed as he recognised the man leading them and instinctively he moved his mount closer to hers.

'Madame la Marquise, this is an unexpected pleasure.' James reined in and touched his bonnet respectfully.

She acknowledged him with a faint nod of her head, wanting to make it clear she had not forgotten his previous behaviour and was not pleased to have him interrupt her ride.

'It is certainly unexpected,' she answered, looking questioningly at the lathered horses of the men about her. They had been riding hard for several hours—hunting perhaps? Animal or man?

James had not glanced once at Jean-Paul, but he was only too aware of the protective way he had edged his horse close to Isabel's. Protecting her from what? he wondered. Why should he be concerned they had been seen—unless—— His eyes swept towards Craeg Riabhach then returned to Isabel's hostile face, his mind suddenly filled with suspicion.

'Have you been riding long?'

'Several hours—as you have,' Isabel answered coolly. 'Did you have a hard chase? Your horses look exhausted.'

'Our quarry eluded us, as successfully today as he has for the past year,' James said in a hard tone. He motioned to the man at his side who wore the colours of the Clan MacKay. 'My steward sighted him just after dawn this morning.'

Isabel's hands tightened so fiercely over the reins in her grasp that the knuckles showed white. With an effort she controlled the cold anger surging through her.

'You have been hunting my brother,' she breathed, 'like an animal.'

'Like the cold-blooded murderer he is,' James retorted.

Blind hatred swept away Isabel's composure. Jean-Paul saw the sudden change in her and was alarmed. The last time he had witnessed such animosity in her eyes had been at the funeral of her husband—that was the last time she had shown any emotion whatsoever—and now this arrogant Highlander had somehow managed to rouse her back to reality.

'Madame.' He laid a gentle hand on her arm, trying in a subtle way to warn her of the pitfall ahead. The last thing she wanted was to reveal her love for Duncan in front of the very man who had vowed to bring him to justice.

She did not even hear him. She only had eyes for James MacLeod.

'Nothing has been proved against my brother, certainly not the charge of murder.'

'You seem to forget there were two witnesses to the crime, Malcolm and his steward, Andrew Beaton.' A tight smile tugged at the corners of James's mouth. 'He will be interested to hear you question his story.'

'If you kill Duncan,' Isabel said slowly, 'I'll have you hunted down in the same manner.'

James's gaze held hers. Somehow he knew it was no idle threat. She was angry, but not hysterical, and the way she was looking at him forced him to acknowledge she was capable of such an act. Contemptuously he moved his gaze to Jean-Paul's motionless figure.

'By him?'

'I have sufficient money to buy a dozen assassins.' Isabel's moment of agitation was past and her voice was once more perfectly controlled. Why she had allowed this man to upset her she would never know. The sight of him alone had been enough to send her into a near-panic.

'I will gladly save Madame the trouble of looking elsewhere,' the Frenchman intervened.

James swore under his breath.

'If you had shown such concern for your husband, Madame la Marquise, he might have lived a little longer—or perhaps you grew bored with him as you seem to do with everything else——'

Too late he saw the riding crop in Isabel's upraised hand, and even Jean-Paul's outstretched hand, meant to restrain her, came a full minute after the blow had been struck. The cane caught James across the right cheek so fiercely that blood began to flow immediately. As he reeled back, Isabel urged her horse into a gallop and pushed past him. Jean-Paul's hesitation was only momentary. He could settle with the Highlander for his insults at another time, his first concern was to protect his mistress.

As he wheeled his horse to follow, the nearest man began moving forward as if to stop him. The flat of Jean-Paul's hand against his chest sent him reeling backwards and gave him the necessary advantage.

James felt blood on his fingers as he touched his cheek. Without diverting any attention from the two fleeing riders he ordered harshly:

'Bring them back—but no one is to lay a sword or hand on the woman.'

An appreciative growl ran through his men as they realised that the man had not been included in the order. Had James not been so explicit they would have killed both for daring to attack their chief.

'My lord, take this.' James's steward, Bran MacKay, held out a piece of cloth which James took and gingerly wiped his cheek.

'My God, there was some force in that blow. I don't think the Marquise is too fond of me, Bran.'

'You can hardly blame her for that—young Duncan was her favourite.'

'I thought so, too, but since her return she's done her damnedest to change my mind. What game is she playing, I wonder?'

'I've heard she seeks only to satisfy her female appetite,' Bran said contemptuously. 'You would do well to remember what she is, my lord, before becoming involved with her.'

'You are my friend as well as my steward,' James said, looking at the man who had been raised with him since childhood, 'but you are not my keeper. The lovely Marquise owes me an apology—at the very least.'

James spurred his horse on to where his men had encircled Isabel and Jean-Paul and brought them to a halt. He caught sight of the Frenchman's sword half-raised at the nearest MacLeod and heard Isabel's cry.

'No, Jean-Paul! Put away your weapon or they will kill you.'

'How wise of you.' James reined in at her side with a satisfied smile, unperturbed by the anger on her face, it no longer bothered him. 'Tell your servant to sheath his sword and ride peacefully with my men, or it will be the worse for him.'

'Ride where?' Isabel demanded.

'To sample the hospitality of De'n Ceo.'

'Don't trust him, Madame,' Jean-Paul said hoarsely.

'You need not fear for your mistress's safety, I'm not about to abduct her,' James mocked, adding in a harder tone: 'Though if it was my intention there would be nothing you could do about it, and if you tried I'd still take her and leave you dead behind me.'

'There have been men before you who have found I am not an easy man to kill,' Jean-Paul flung back challengingly.

'Do not provoke him.' Isabel spoke in French, grateful for this link with the man at her side which gave them an advantage over the MacLeods surrounding them. 'We will do as he says without a fight.'

'What if he suspects our motives for being in this area?'

'He may suspect, but he has no proof—and he will get none.' Turning to James, she asked, 'Shall we go, my lord?'

Ordering three of his men to go ahead and the others to bring up the rear, James motioned her to ride beside him. He had only a slight knowledge of French and had been unable to follow the swift exchange. Once again he found Isabel's association with the arrogant Frenchman irritating him. Here was a woman of rank and great beauty who would have little trouble in attracting any man she chose, yet she preferred to have a servant as a lover.

The ride to De'n Ceo was made in silence. It was Isabel's way of showing her displeasure. As she reined in her horse before the old castle, James was at her side to help her to dismount. He watched her eyes rove over the weathered stones before her and smiled.

'Welcome back to De'n Ceo, Isabel. It's been a long time since you were last here. Why do you look so disdainful? As a little girl you were always Isabel to me.'

'I am a woman now,' Isabel retorted, quickly disengaging herself from his grasp.

'A very bitter one. Can we not be friends—as we were in the old days?'

She turned and looked up into the berry-brown face above her. Friends with the man sworn to hunt down and kill her beloved brother!

'Friends, my lord—with whom? Madame la Marquise de Riché—or Isabel MacLeod who used to run barefoot through the heather?'

'Have you changed so much?'

'When I was a child I used to believe in good fairies and beasties—now I know only the beasties exist. My husband, men like him—like you, who look at me and see only a woman of easy virtue.'

'The girl I remember was a wild little tomboy who could outrun and outswim all of us in the glen. The only one you couldn't outride was me. Many things have changed since you went away—the failure of the uprising brought more than just poverty. Sometimes it is pleasant to dwell on childhood days when our lives were uncomplicated.'

If only she could believe he was speaking the truth, and there was no ulterior motive behind this show of friendliness. She took the arm he offered and walked through the high arched doorway into the castle.

Inside it was cool and shadowy. When she was a girl, De'n Ceo had always fascinated her, but she had never ventured within sight of it without the company of one or other of her brothers, fearful of the demons and beasties Lachlan warned guarded the old place. The Gaelic name meant 'of the mist' and it was aptly named. On a summer's day it was like a fairy castle with the mists rolling away from it as the first sun's rays slanted down upon the stonework, and the high turrets seemed to stretch upwards as if reaching for the clouds. But in winter the heavy clinging mists wrapped themselves around it like a protective cloak, shielding it from the outside world, and it was rumoured old ghosts patrolled the walls—ghastly visitations of ancient Norsemen who had invaded and died at the castle gates for so many years, before the chief of one of the raiding galleys had been sorely wounded and tended by the daughter of the MacLeod.

He had ended up by marrying her and taking her father's name. Many of his people had settled in the glen and intermarriage had mingled the bloods of wild Norsemen and fierce Highlanders. That same blood now ran through the veins of James MacLeod, Isabel thought.

In the great hall she saw there were wine and glasses already set out on the table and her lips tightened determinedly as James led her to a chair.

'If we are to be friends, you must accept the woman you see before you now,' she said, turning to face him.

'I see, Isabel MacLeod, that the tomboy has been replaced by a very beautiful woman, and I would be a liar if I said I was not attracted to you. Does that offend you?'

'A woman likes to be admired, but I would prefer it to go no further.'

'Then we are friends?'

Isabel held out her hand with a slight nod and he touched his lips to her fingers with a smile. Over her shoulder, he caught sight of Jean-Paul lingering in the doorway and said quietly:

'Then there is no longer need for your bodyguard to remain.'

Isabel flushed at the undercurrent of mockery in his tone. She glanced towards the silent figure.

'You need not wait, Jean-Paul—I shall be quite safe.'

'Madame might require something. I will remain in the outer room—within call should you need me.'

Isabel saw James's lips tighten as he bowed and turned on his heel.

'Are all your servants as wilful as that one?'

'Jean-Paul and his sister have served me well, I have no complaints,' Isabel answered. She knew he believed the Frenchman to be her lover—Malcolm would have convinced him of that—but she remained silent and began to look expectantly around the room.

'We are quite alone,' James murmured. 'Are you thinking you need a chaperon after all?'

'Your mother——' Isabel began.

'She died over two years ago.'

'I'm sorry, I didn't know.' Taking the glass of brandy he held out to her, she moved to the window and looked out across the Atlantic. 'The last time I stood here I was ten years old. It was the night of your birthday party, do you remember? I was under strict instructions from Father to be on my best behaviour. Duncan and I grew bored with being ignored and went exploring. Somehow we became separated and your mother found me in one of the upstairs rooms. She was very beautiful, wasn't she—and she loved beautiful things, too. She showed me her dresses and her jewellery, and while everyone danced and drank down here we sat in her boudoir and she talked of magic castles and the "Green Mantle". Is it really true what she told me—or was it only a tale to intrigue a child?'

With a smile, James took her glass and put it aside. 'Come with me.'

He led her up the wide wooden staircase, flanked on either side by ornately carved handrails, to the first floor. As she followed him along the corridor Isabel was once more ten years old, in her first grown-up dress of blue satin, following behind an elegantly gowned woman whose ball-gown of some wispy material flowed out around her like a fairy cloak. Her voice came out of the shadows as soft and gentle as the quiet ripple of water on a summer's day.

Isabel had been completely overawed by this splendid figure, who had come upon her wandering through the castle and instead of reproaching her had stayed to talk and had told her of the many places in the castle where a child could hide and never be found—as James did when he was naughty. And Isabel had laughed to think of James MacLeod hiding because of a misdemeanour.

The memories of the woman became clearer as her companion opened a door and stood back for her to enter. She stepped into a large room brilliant with sunshine flooding through the windows. The first time she had been here, the room had been lit by a single candelabrum standing on a brass-topped table, and she had sat on the edge of the four-poster bed.

Nothing had changed. The table and the lamp still remained—as did the pale yellow bedcover and the embroidered pillows. The rooms downstairs were comfortable, but typically the abode of a man, without the touch of a woman to soften their hardness. Here, everything was feminine and lavish, as if Lady MacLeod still lived. Isabel moved slowly around the room, often touching a certain object as another recollection returned, and wondered at the great love James still had for his mother. Why else would her rooms remain untouched?

She felt James's arm brush hers as he stepped past her towards the bed and saw the undisguised pain in his eyes as he touched one of the embroidered pillows.

'She never got over my father's death. She used to sit in this very room—over there on the window seat—watching the sea as if she expected him to come back at any time. I couldn't understand why my love wasn't enough and one day I broached her about it. All she said was—"When you fall in love you will love as I do, because you are of my flesh and blood and then you will understand how I feel".'

'And have you?'

'No—and I hope to God I never do. Her life ended when my father died. No one person should demand such a sacrifice from another.'

'It wasn't demanded,' Isabel broke in quietly. 'She gave herself freely. I think she must have known something wonderful. What happened to her?'

'She went to stay with relatives near Dunvegan for a while. On the return journey the boat sank in a storm on the Minch. There were no survivors. These rooms have been left as they are on her instructions. She used to say that after she was gone she would like my wife to have them and spend as many happy years in them as she had. I've respected her wishes—but it will be a rare woman who inherits all this. You are the first to enter them since her death, apart from her maid who still cares for them as meticulously as she did in the old days.'

'Your mother was a very rare woman, too. Like De'n Ceo, she had a magic way about her.'

'She named this place. She said this castle "was of the mist"—so was love. One moment it enveloped you, the next it slipped through your fingers.'

From the wall closet James took what looked like a folded woollen shawl. As he unfolded it Isabel knew instinctively this was the famous 'Green Mantle' she had been told about. Into it was woven the blue of the sky on a summer's day, the pale blue-green of the sea, the grey and brown and black of the mountains and the purple pink of the heather.

James caressed the woven cloth lovingly as he said, 'She came from a small fishing village near Dunvegan. Women of that village are renowned for the "green mantles" they weave for their menfolk. They are said to protect them from harm in battle. My mother wove this for my father soon after their wedding. In the uprising he wore it, but just before the last battle we fought he gave it to me. He was wounded and died in my arms—I sustained not even a scratch. Until that moment I'd never believed in the mantle—sometimes I still find it hard——' He broke off and, pushing it back into the closet, quickly slammed the door as if to shut away all painful memories as well.

'It was to have been a wedding present to my ward, Kirsty. Who told you about her murder?' He wheeled on her without warning and Isabel found herself under close scrutiny. How swiftly his moods changed, she thought—he would be a difficult man to deceive.

'Mary. She was the only one willing to discuss it.'

'Then you didn't come back to help Duncan?'

'That's the second time you have asked that of me. You're right in thinking I knew there was trouble before I came home—Lachlan wrote and told me that Duncan had killed a girl in a jealous rage. He asked me to return for my father's sake.'

'And you came despite the bitterness between you?'

'We are of the same blood.'

'I almost believe you,' James muttered.

Isabel gave a soft amused laugh.

'I don't care whether you do or not. What's wrong, James—is your conscience bothering you?'

He looked at her with a frown darkening his handsome features.

'And what's that supposed to mean?'

'I know what my father did for you after the uprising. You owed him more than your life. Was Kirsty Fraser payment of your debt?'

James came across the room at her like an unleashed tiger. She could not only see his fury, but feel it as he came to a halt only inches from her, demanding harshly. Instinctively she knew she had made a wild guess and come near to the truth.

'It isn't in my nature to use people.'

'But you used her, didn't you?' Isabel prompted quietly. 'And you chided me for my disloyalty to Duncan! We are no longer children—our lives took separate paths, thanks to Malcolm, and now Duncan is a murderer and I can do nothing to help him. But if he is caught, James MacLeod, what I told you will happen—I shall avenge him. That at least I will be able to do.' She smiled and dropped a polite, mocking curt-sey before him. 'I thank you for your brandy and the unexpected hospitality, but it is time for me to leave.'

As she turned towards the door James stepped in front of her, barring the way. He was pale and visibly shaking with what she could only imagine was anger. Was she the first person to guess his secret?

'You'll go when I say so, you bitch.'

'Insults? Don't worry, James, I won't tell anyone else. You can continue to suffer alone.'

For a moment James stared down into the beautiful, mocking face before him, then with a low oath he reached out and caught hold of her. The hard pressure of his mouth on hers stopped Isabel's protest before it was uttered and shocked her into silence. She knew she should fight him—thrust her clenched fist into his face and stop him crushing her against his broad chest before his opinion of her reputation was confirmed by her acquiescence. But she was suddenly aroused by the contact of a man's body against hers after so long—hard, warm, masterful. So different from Julian, but far more dangerous. He could destroy not only her body, but her very soul.

His forcefulness parted her stiff lips and transported her to a world she had never known before—and never wanted to leave. A kiss from her husband had never brought such ecstasy, and fear ran through her like quicksilver. Pulling her mouth free, she pushed down at the hands around her body—James released her with-out argument. His eyes narrowed to derisive slits as he asked cruelly:

'Did you earn your reputation with boys? My God, you've never been kissed by a real man before.'

'I look forward to the first time,' Isabel returned bitingly.

He stepped back and opening the door motioned to the corridor.

'You can go now. I'm sorry if I offended you. It was not my intention.'

'You made your intentions quite clear the other night.'

'I'm glad we understand each other,' James answered, 'it will save all this preliminary nonsense the next time.'

Isabel went white as the full meaning of his words struck her. For a moment she contemplated striking him, then realising it would be a meaningless gesture, she turned and left him, struggling to retain her composure as she heard him step out behind to watch her descend the staircase.

'I've decided to go to Inverness tomorrow,' Isabel said unexpectedly as Simone was brushing her hair. It was late afternoon and she had been sleeping soundly since her return to Asher Mor at a fierce gallop, her mouth still stinging from James MacLeod's kisses.

'Inverness, Madame—so soon after your arrival here?'

Simone looked at her quizzically, noting the flushed cheeks and the agitation in her mistress's eyes, but wisely making no comment. Jean-Paul had told her of their visit to De'n Ceo, and both were wondering what had taken place while Isabel was alone with the MacLeod. Simone had not seen her so restless for many months, and now this sudden idea to go away seemed to confirm her growing suspicions. 'Shall I inform Jean-Paul and have him order a carriage for the morning?'

'He isn't going with us—I'm sending him to France, Simone, to sell the town house. The furniture is to come here, to help restore this old barn to the comfort it once knew. The money from the sale I will give to my father—he badly needs it.'

'It sounds a good idea, you never did like that place, but why must we go to Inverness?'

'Where else can I find materials for new clothes and presents for my family? I came home empty-handed, remember—it's time I bought a few little things,' Isabel returned, rising to her feet at the sound of a knock at the door. 'That will be Jean-Paul. Let him in and then you can go to the Lady Mary—I believe she wants you to dress her hair in one of the Paris styles, doesn't she?'

Simone nodded. She was growing accustomed to being loaned to Mary MacLeod for various odd jobs. She did not mind, for it gave her a chance to mix with the other maids and listen to the latest gossip. She opened the door and smiled briefly at her brother before closing it and going out.

'Pour yourself a drink, Jean-Paul, and sit down, I won't be a moment.' Isabel motioned to her sitting-room and the decanter of wine and glasses on the table. 'I will have one too.'

She missed the searching look he directed at her. When she joined him, he was standing in the middle of the room, holding a glass for her.

'Thank you, Jean-Paul. Well, are you ready to leave tomorrow?'

'Yes, Madame—as you said, one of the local fishermen is willing to take me across.'

'Good—I want the house sold with all speed. Get a good price, but don't haggle.' She held out a sheaf of papers. 'Here is my authorisation for the sale and a letter to the solicitors in Paris telling them to deal with you in all things, and everything else you will need.' She broke off with an annoyed exclamation as the door opened and Malcolm came unannounced into the room. Her lips tightened at the sight of the derisive smile which sprang to his eyes at the sight of Jean-Paul.

'Am I interrupting something?'

'A private conversation. What do you want, Malcolm?'

'Your maid—Mary tells me she is to attend her.'

'Simone left here some while ago. If you had just left Mary, you would know she is with her. What is it you really want?'

'You went riding early this morning—I'd like to know where?'

'Not that it's any of your business, but I rode as far as Sandwood and then came home—by way of De'n Ceo.'

An unpleasant chuckle rose in Malcolm's throat and his gaze raked the elegantly groomed woman before him.

'So that's why you were so long. I wondered how long it would be before you took up with James. Enjoy yourself while you can, Isabel, because he's using you to get to Duncan. We both know why you really came back.'

Isabel shrugged her slim shoulders and sipped at her wine with a deliberate indifference meant to anger her brother.

'You can both believe what you like. As for finding James MacLeod attractive enough to go to his bed, you're wrong about that, too. As a matter of fact I find this place and the men here as boring as the grave—tomorrow I'm off to Inverness.'

She was sure she glimpsed a hint of relief in Malcolm's eyes before he swung away, muttering that she was willing to find her pleasures elsewhere.

'You have a persuasive tongue, I almost believed you myself,' Jean-Paul said softly as the door slammed.

Isabel felt her cheeks burn with embarrassment at the inference behind the words.

'What are you suggesting, Jean-Paul?' She tried to sound disinterested, but already the memory of what had taken place earlier that day was returning, and her voice faltered and broke.

'James MacLeod is an attractive man,' the French-man said meaningly.

'Yes—yes he is,' Isabel stammered.

'You were surrounded by such men in Versailles and not one of them was interested in anything but getting you to bed.'

'I know, but that hasn't made me hope some day a man will feel something different for me.' She spun around and he was shocked by the sight of the bright tears sparkling in her eyes. 'My body has been sold to save the honour of the family name, used and defiled by an old man who hated me. Every man who ever looked at me has stripped me naked with his eyes. My name has been bandied through Versailles as the source of dirty jokes. Just once, Jean-Paul, only once, I want to look into a man's eyes and discover that I am a woman. I've been denied love—starved of affection. Is it any wonder I'm afraid of James MacLeod—afraid of myself and what might happen if I allow him to touch me?'

She cried out as Jean-Paul grasped her by the shoulders and roughly shook her.

'Look into my eyes, Isabel de Riché—see the woman mirrored there. The beautiful, uncomplicated woman who rules my heart.' He gave a harsh laugh at the sight of the shocked expression on her face. 'You've known how I feel for months, perhaps I should have spoken before——'

'No, Jean-Paul—no!' Isabel tried to pull free of his grasp, but she was held fast and helpless. As he pulled her against his chest she could hear the fierce thudding of his heart. She was frightened, yet she became still as he fastened a hand in her loose hair and tugged back her head. She was as helpless against him as she had been against the man who had grabbed hold of her so force-fully only a few hours before. She closed her eyes against the passion blazing out of his face and immedi-

ately another face swam before the mists of her mind.
The kisses rained on her mouth came from another—a
man she had denied—they brought her almost to
insensibility and she sagged, spent and breathless, in
the arms which held her.

'No—no—James—no!'

Through reeling senses she felt herself lifted backwards and carried into the other room, and then the feel
of the silken bedcover beneath her. When she opened
her eyes she was alone, and only then did she realise
what she had said.

When Simone returned, Isabel ordered a bath to be
prepared. The maid looked questioningly at the girl's
tearful face and the dishevelled state of her dress, but
Isabel offered no explanation. Hours later, when she
was composed, she sent for Jean-Paul on the pretext of
wanting to give him fresh instructions before he left for
France. He did not come. Simone was sent to find him.
She returned to say he had left Asher Mor early that
evening.

'Did you pass on my message?' Isabel asked of the silent
woman staring out at the passing countryside.

'Yes, Madame,' Simone answered. 'I slipped out of
the house before anyone was awake and went to the
house of Donald Dhu as you instructed. He said to tell
you it would reach your brother by noon.'

Isabel looked up into the cloudless sky. It was past
midday—if all had gone well Duncan would have the
news of her departure to Inverness and so would not
risk going near Asher Mor to try to contact her.

When she returned, a ball might be the perfect
opportunity to gain the odd piece of information while
tongues were loosened by an abundance of wine and
spirits—she would see to it there was more than enough
to ensure that happened. The men would bring their

womenfolk—some of whom would surely have known Kirsty Fraser, and there would be at least one eager to relate the sad tale.

If only she had not had the misunderstanding with Jean-Paul, Isabel thought sadly. There was nothing to keep him with her now. If he ever returned to Scotland their relationship could never be the same again.

CHAPTER
FOUR

ISABEL remained in Inverness for over a month—far longer than she intended—but she found the house enchanting and at once set about refurnishing it. She lived quietly during the four weeks, making no attempt to entertain or to get to know her neighbours, and spent most of her time enjoying the peace of her new surroundings.

It was Simone who tactfully reminded her of her father and Asher Mor and brought Isabel once more face to face with the great responsibility she had taken upon herself. After collecting the last of the new dresses she had had made from the dressmaker, she gave orders for the house to be closed up and preparations made for the journey home.

As the carriage turned into the courtyard of Asher Mor, the sight which greeted Isabel made her lean forward in her seat and catch Simone by the arm, her eyes alight with excitement.

'Look! The furniture has arrived, Jean-Paul didn't let me down after all.'

'When has he ever done that?' the maid demanded in a suspicious tone.

'Never—I mean, I didn't expect it to arrive so quickly.' Isabel returned quickly. She had said nothing to Simone about the incident with Jean-Paul, afraid that it might upset the closeness of their relationship also. 'Oh, Simone, isn't it good to see it again—the house I hated, but I furnished it myself. It will be nice to have my own things around me again.'

Everything except the bed in which she had spent her

honeymoon, Simone thought, casting an eye over the various items stacked each side of the main doors. Isabel was out of the coach the moment it stopped, pulling aside the protective covers to make an inspection.

'There's more in here, mistress, we've left it all until ye came back to know where ye want it put.' Lachlan met her in the Great Hall and waved a hand at the huge gold-framed mirrors and the dozens of paintings lining the walls. 'The master thinks ye have taken leave of your senses,' he added with a wry smile.

'And you, Lachlan—what do you think?' Isabel asked with a laugh.

'Ye made him happy by coming home—to restore the old place to some of its former glory will let an old man die not only happy but proud.'

'Die!' Isabel's smile faded. 'Tell me the truth—as my true friend—how ill is he?'

'Another attack like the one he had a few weeks before you came will most certainly kill him. He is living on the time you have given him, mistress, and I bless ye for it.'

'Thank you, Lachlan.' Isabel glanced at the array of objects around her. 'What did he say when he saw all this?'

'He says ye have gone a little mad in the head, but it would have done ye heart good to see the way his eyes lighted up when he first saw it.'

'Good! Let me go and change and bathe and then I will tell you where everything is to go. Ask the Lady Mary to come to my apartment if she can spare a moment.'

Isabel was disappointed to discover that Jean-Paul was not at Asher Mor. As she lazed in a warm bath she had visions of him enjoying the money he had obtained from the sale of the house in some tavern off the

Pont-Neuf. Even Simone voiced her surprise at his absence.

Isabel was unable to keep her secret any longer. The maid listened in a stony-faced silence and made no comment when she had finished. Who did she blame, Isabel wondered—herself or her brother?

Mary came into the bedroom as Isabel was studying a list of the items which had arrived and wondering where to put it all. She required only a few pieces for her own rooms.

'Lachlan said you wanted to see me.' Mary stood before her chair and seemed uneasy. 'Is it important? I'm rather busy at the moment trying to sort out how many guests are coming for the ball.'

'Good heavens, I'd forgotten I mentioned it to Father. Has he sent out the invitations already?'

'Two days after you left. He expected you back earlier, you know. The ball is the day after tomorrow. He was beginning to think you might not be here—and now we have all this furniture to clear away—Really, Isabel, you might have given me some warning!'

Isabel's eyes narrowed at the animosity in the other woman's voice. When she went away they had been friends.

'It was intended as a surprise—the same way Father intended the ball to be for me. Why are you angry, Mary? Is it me—have I done something wrong?'

'What could Isabel MacLeod do wrong in Asher Mor?' Mary asked cuttingly. 'Whatever you were in France, here you are the mistress of the house again, while I—I am nothing. The servants no longer consult me about anything.'

'Then you should speak to Malcolm about it. I did not come back to take your place. From what I have seen you manage very effectively without my help.'

'Malcolm thinks the situation to be highly amusing,' Mary returned with a brittle laugh.

'He has not lost his warped sense of humour.' Isabel rose from her chair and caught Mary by the hands, despite her attempt to move away. 'You are a full-grown woman, not a child, Mary. Assert your authority—demand the respect due to you as my brother's wife. If the servants look to me for orders, you cannot blame them, this was my home long before you came. They must see we are friends and in agreement in all things. I shall make it known they are to come to you for their orders as in the past. Are we friends?'

Mary's face flushed with colour. Malcolm's derisive remarks on her inability to run the house had brought her to Isabel's room in a quarrelsome frame of mind.

'Could we not run the house together——' she began and broke off as Isabel shook her head.

'One mistress is sufficient, but if you need me, I will always be here. Now—the furniture, that's why I wanted to see you. Before I have Lachlan start moving it, I thought you might like to select some pieces for your own use.'

'Could I? Oh, Isabel, that would be wonderful—my rooms are so bare. Oh, dear—I didn't mean to sound discontented, but there hasn't been any money to buy extra little things to make the place more comfortable.'

'I understand. Go downstairs and choose what you want. In the meantime I'll finish sorting out the invitations if you wish.'

'Thank you, I'd much prefer you to do it. The ball is so close and I'm still trying to arrange the kitchen.'

'So long as there is plenty to drink the evening will be a huge success,' Isabel laughed. 'Half the men Father has invited will probably be old family friends—drinking friends that is. Off with you now and see to the furniture. I'll meet you in the library in half an hour and we'll arrange the menu.'

*   *   *

For the remainder of the day, Isabel did not have a moment to herself. There was the food to be discussed with Mary—the table arrangements and the seating of the guests, which totalled more than a hundred. People had been invited from as far as Lochinver and there were less than half a dozen refusals, and then there was the decorating of the banquet room for the occasion. It had not been used since her marriage, Lachlan told her as she surveyed the long bleak room. It had four large french windows opening out on to a courtyard and a minimum of unimpressive furniture. Determinedly, Isabel began selecting pieces to be moved in and paintings for the bare walls—after that she was not satisfied until every scrap of the furniture had found a new home somewhere in Asher Mor. She was greatly rewarded for all her efforts by Lachlan's enthusiasm as they inspected the rooms late that evening—yet still a part of her could not feel glad. Without Jean-Paul her world was not complete.

Early next morning she went riding alone. Only a few of the servants had seen her leave, but she was still cautious in case Malcolm or his steward had been spying on her, and for more than two hours she rode at a leisurely pace with no apparent destination in mind, then, satisfied she had not been followed, she turned her horse in the direction of Craeg Riabhach, the mountain which sheltered her brother from his enemies.

As the gentle slopes became steeper, she tethered her horse beneath a full-branched tree and continued on, aware as she did so of a sudden stillness in the air. She was being watched. She could feel a dozen pairs of eyes on her as she continued to climb, and then out of a narrow crevice in the side of the sheer rocky face above her squeezed a familiar figure, sliding down to meet her with an eagerness that made her break into a breathless run.

'Duncan! Oh, Duncan!'

Enfolded in her brother's strong arms, her head against his shoulder, Isabel forgot Asher Mor and the elder brother who wanted so much to kill the man who held her—forgot the vow of James MacLeod and the danger she herself would be in if it was discovered she was Duncan's ally.

From all sides came silent men, their grave faces softening slightly at the sight of the embracing couple. Weapons were sheathed and one by one they climbed up to squeeze—some not without great difficulty—through the narrow opening from which their leader had appeared.

Isabel's fingers trembled as she touched a new scar on Duncan's left cheek.

'You've been hurt.'

'A slight encounter with some of James's men—but I got away. I'm afraid they might know of this hiding-place, however—there have been men searching this area for the past week.'

While she was in Inverness in safety and comfort, Isabel thought with a pang of conscience.

'I've let you down—I've found out nothing,' she began miserably, but was interrupted by Duncan's hand against her mouth.

'You could never let me down, little one. Hold fast to my hand now and I'll show you my new home. It may not have the comforts of Asher Mor, but it's a damn' sight safer.'

Tightly grasping her brother's wrist, Isabel followed him up the slope. She had forgotten how strong he was—he lifted her over rocks and uneven ground with effortless ease. He had taught her to climb as a child and they had spent many happy hours exploring the caves and mountains around Cape Wrath. With the warm sun on her face and the reassuring grasp of Duncan's hand on hers, she was transported for a moment back to those wonderful times.

'Mind the rock here, it's as sharp as a knife-edge,' Duncan murmured, and she came out of her dream and stepped carefully after him into a long pass-way honeycombed with caves. A meagre amount of light came from an opening in the rocks high above them, but the main source blazed from the many wall torches. The opening she had just come through was too small to allow the light to be seen outside and was as well hidden a crevice she doubted if it could be seen at all from below.

She passed through two small caves, one with a few blankets thrown down on the floor, the other filled with food and weapons, to a larger one at the far end of the passageway where Duncan's men were seated around a fire or lounging on roughly fashioned beds.

'Go down to the lower slopes and make sure my sister wasn't followed,' Duncan ordered one of them. With a smile he drew Isabel down beside him on his own pallet of blankets, asking, 'What do you think of my inheritance?'

'Duncan—it's terrible—you're living the way our ancestors used to. Isn't there any justice in the world?'

'There will be when I bring Malcolm to account for Kirsty's murder. Don't look so worried, little sister, my men and I are used to it—as for the fact you have discovered nothing new to clear me, I didn't expect you to just yet. Malcolm is no doubt suspicious of you, and from what I hear James MacLeod kept you occupied before you went to Inverness.'

The colour flamed into his sister's cheeks so violently Duncan began to laugh. 'Why, I do believe you're taken with him.'

Isabel swallowed the angry retort which rose to her lips. She had promised herself that no one would provoke her over a man she disliked and distrusted.

'I've told him that if he hunts you down I'll have him killed the same way,' she declared.

Duncan looked concerned at the vehemence in her voice.

'Don't make an enemy of James because of me. You have your own life to lead.'

'Don't be silly, I wouldn't look twice at him,' Isabel returned with forced lightness. 'Duncan, listen to me—I've bought a house in Inverness under the name of Isabel de Bray. I thought using Mother's maiden name would prevent the asking of any awkward questions. It's completely furnished now, and I've installed a permanent housekeeper with instructions to be prepared for a visit from me at any time—or from my brother who lives in France but occasionally makes business trips to Scotland. You can go there any time you wish. See, here—I have brought you money for clothes,' she fumbled in the pocket of her riding coat and brought out a small leather purse.

'There are also a few items of jewellery you could sell if you run short. Go there, please, Duncan—I can hardly sleep at night for fear Malcolm will come hammering at my door with news of your capture.'

'And my men, Isabel? They have shared so much with me. Can I go to Inverness and live in comfort while they live like animals?'

'If you are caught they will live this way for the rest of their lives,' Isabel protested. 'Only by proving your innocence can you free yourself and them. If I have any news I will send word or come myself.'

'Inverness is a fair distance should you need help. But then I'm forgetting you have that French bodyguard watching over you—I'll go, then, for a few days at least. It will be good to sleep in a comfortable bed again and not fear a dirk in my back.'

Isabel paled lightly at the reference to Jean-Paul, but

knowing Duncan would not leave if she told him she was alone, she wisely kept silent.

'Promise me you won't antagonise Malcolm,' Duncan begged. 'If he suspects you are trying to help me, we both know he'll have no compunction about killing you.'

'What about his steward, Andrew Beaton?' Isabel asked. 'Can he be bought?'

'You'll be treading on dangerous ground there, little one. Once you approach him he'll know of your intentions. He's a greedy, ambitious swine, but he could still accept your money and turn you over to Malcolm.'

'I'll be careful, I promise.' Regretfully Isabel rose to her feet. 'I mustn't stay any longer—I expect you've heard about the ball tonight.'

'The whole glen has been talking of it for weeks,' Duncan answered, an arm around her shoulders as they walked back towards the entrance. 'What wouldn't I give to be with you tonight—to dance with the most attractive woman Asher Mor has ever seen.'

'Dear Duncan, it will be that way again soon.' Isabel held him close for a long moment, then, with a brief kiss, she slipped out of the cave and scrambled quickly down the mountainside to where her horse was tethered, afraid that at the last moment her composure might break and she would give way to tears.

Isabel's dress for the ball was one she had had made for her début at Versailles. It had not been worn since that night when she had dazzled the court with her beauty—a tall, slender creature in shimmering white lace, the bodice and skirt sewn with hundreds of tiny diamonds, the sleeves slashed with scarlet velvet bows. A set of six matching diamonds had adorned the thick chignon of blonde hair.

As she stared at the same reflection in the full-length mirror in her sitting-room, Isabel was back in France,

walking through the crowded ballroom on the arm of
her ageing bridegroom to be presented to the King and
Queen. How thrilled she had been—how excited, not
knowing that soon the society which welcomed her into
their midst as the new Marquise de Riché would brand
her as a whore, using her presence among them as a
source of malicious gossip.

As she descended the stairs to the Great Hall, James
MacLeod and her father came through the open doors.
The latter was holding on to the arm of the younger
man, and Isabel felt a pang of resentment at the close
bond between them which made it possible for James to
come and go from Asher Mor without an invitation.

'Isabel, my child, how exquisite you look.' The
pride on Alistair's face thrust the unwelcome feeling
out of her mind and she took his other arm with a
smile.

'Good evening, Isabel.' James's dark eyes, full of
unspoken mockery, examined her from head to toe.

He was challenging her to remember what had taken
place at their last meeting, she thought—as if she could
forget.

'James and I are going to have a quiet drink together
in the drawing-room. Before you go and greet the guests
which have already arrived,' Alistair said, 'Lachlan
tells me that that French servant of yours has returned
and wishes a private word with you in the library.'

'Jean-Paul—here! But that's wonderful——' Isabel
broke off at the disapproving expression on her
father's face. He would never know why his words had
given her such pleasure. Taking her leave of him, she
picked up her skirts and almost ran to the library
door.

'Jean-Paul!'

The Frenchman turned from the window and
instinctively she stepped forward, stretching out her
hands towards him. He clasped them so tightly he hurt

her—then abruptly he kissed them and stepped back, his face expressionless.

'Did you not expect me, Madame?' His tone was faintly insolent. Reminiscent of when he had first joined her household, Isabel thought, feeling the colour rising in her cheeks. 'Perhaps Madame did not expect me to return at all?'

'What reason would you have to desert me?' she asked slowly.

'I gave you reason enough before I went away—or do you need reminding?'

Isabel forced herself to meet his gaze.

'I remember perfectly. I don't blame you for what took place—the fault was mine for ignoring the way you felt. If we had talked perhaps you would not have found it necessary to act—to act so violently. If only we had talked, Jean-Paul, I would never have hurt you so thoughtlessly. The last thing I want is to hurt you, of all people.'

Jean-Paul's mouth tightened at the sight of the tears spilling down over her cheeks. She was trembling too, and he freed his hands as if they had become red-hot.

'I will cause you no further distress, Madame. I have completed your business for you. The house has been sold and I have a banker's draft in my pocket. The furniture has arrived, and I see it has greatly improved the house as you thought. If everything is to your satisfaction, I will take my leave of you. The ship sails tomorrow evening and I would like to be on it.'

'Sails—for where?' Isabel stared at him stupidly —what was he suggesting?

'To France, Madame. Where else? My old tavern is up for sale—I thought I might buy it back.'

'Go back! And Simone?'

'My sister has made it quite plain that she intends to remain with you. She duly reprimanded me for what happened.'

Isabel pressed a hand to her temple which had begun
to throb maddeningly. He was going to leave because
he could not have her for himself! The one man in
whom she placed complete trust. Even the violence of
what had passed between them did not alter that. He
was abandoning her to return to the squalor of his old
life. Taverns and whores, and everything which went
with such things. Faintly she said:

'You can't leave me.'

'If you *need* anyone, may I suggest you turn to James
MacLeod,' came the cruel retort. The eyes which
watched her unmercifully narrowed as her face
blanched. 'Of course, if Madame was to ask me to
stay—as a personal favour...'

His meaning was only too clear. He wanted her to
beg him to stay—to prove she was dependent on
him—to place herself totally in his power. Isabel
turned away, leaning against the mantel for support.
She had never realised the depth of the cruelty in his
untamed nature until this moment. What was she to
do—allow him to go and lose a valued friend? If he
stayed, would he be a friend or a demanding lover?

'Dear God, what am I to do?' Hardly had the whispered words left her lips than she felt Jean-Paul's hands
on her shoulders. She tried to turn, but he held her fast.

'Don't look at me or I shall never say what has to be
said. Forgive me—in a moment of madness I tried to
have what can never be mine. I love you. I worship the
ground you walk on. No—listen to me—we shall never
share such a moment again. Whatever James MacLeod
means to you—it is your affair. It is your right to try
and find a little happiness. *Mon Dieu*, you deserve it.
What happened between us cannot be forgotten, but I
ask you not to hold it against me. Let me stay or send
me away, the decision is yours. If I stay I swear I will
never lay so much as a finger on you again. Things will
be as they were before.'

Isabel turned slowly in his grasp. Her fingers lightly touched the contrite face before her and she smiled through a mist of tears.

'No, it will not be the same—I will never again look on you as a servant. You made me realise the depths of my own feelings, Jean-Paul. It is not the kind of love you feel for me, but it is love—the kind I share with Duncan. Does this offend you? Say it does not. Without you I am lost. No—no, what I ask is impossible.'

'I will be whatever you wish,' Jean-Paul muttered. The fierce light her words had aroused in his eyes slowly died. She could feel the agitation in him as he stood with his hands still resting on her shoulders. Relief flooded through her and she rested her aching forehead on his chest in silent gratitude.

Neither of them noticed the silent figure standing in the half-open doorway, a witness to what appeared to be an embrace between mistress and servant.

'The guests are beginning to look for their hostess,' James drawled, stepping into the room.

They came apart as if a white-hot blade had been thrust between them and the mocking smile on his face masked the surge of blind jealousy which engulfed him. Isabel stood dumbfounded, her cheeks burning fiercely. Without any sign of agitation, Jean-Paul's hands slid from her shoulders. With a slight bow he turned towards the door. He did not even look at James. Isabel came suddenly to life. She, too, ignored the intruder.

'Wait, Jean-Paul, let me take your arm. You must stay and enjoy the ball. Simone will be down later on, and it will be like old times.'

They left James standing in the deserted library, a dangerous glitter in his pale eyes.

In the early hours of the following morning, the last of the guests departed and Isabel assisted her tired but jubilant father to his room. Breathless though he was as he climbed the stairs, he continued to tell her how satisfied he was with the ball and of the high praises sung in respect of the elegant hostess who had prepared everything with such meticulous care.

'That was Mary's doing, Father, not mine, and I think you should tell her how pleased you are.'

'You never did take any credit—even as a child,' Alistair murmured, pausing at the door. Taking Isabel's face in both hands he kissed her on both cheeks.

'Thank you for making an old man very happy. Goodnight, my child.'

'Goodnight, Father.'

Isabel stood in the dark passageway for a long moment, listening to the sound of low voices below as the servants cleared the banquet hall, before continuing on to her room. A welcoming fire blazed in the hearth and Simone was turning down the bedclothes.

'You look tired, *mignonne*.' The maid pulled up a stool before the fire and Isabel sat down with a grateful smile.

'A little, perhaps, but I don't feel like going to bed yet. There's no need for you to wait up, Simone. If you will first unfasten my dress, I can manage the rest myself. I want to sit here and think for a while.'

'Jean-Paul tells me you have come to an understanding,' Simone murmured as she began to unhook Isabel's white gown. 'Don't you think it unwise for him to remain here under the circumstances?'

'Because he is in love with me? No, I don't.'

'My brother can be very possessive when he wishes,' Simone said with a faint frown. 'What if you fall in love under his very nose?'

'There is no man here who interests me,' Isabel answered, but even as she spoke she knew it was a lie. There was one—whose name she dared not speak. He was growing possessive too, and frighteningly confident of himself—or was he sure of *her*?

For a long while after Simone had gone she sat by the fire, remembering childhood days of Asher Mor with Duncan. The roar of the sea outside the window drowned the sound of the bedroom door opening and closing and she was not aware of anyone in the room until a shadow slanted across the hearth, and she looked up with a sharp intake of breath.

James MacLeod stood beside the stool, the aroma of whisky even stronger on him than it had been when they had danced. His eyes lingered on the soft cloud of golden hair which she had unpinned and now fell around her bare shoulders and then slowly dropped to the unfastened ball-gown.

'It appears I was expected,' he drawled sardonically.

Isabel sprang to her feet with the colour flooding into her cheeks.

'How dare you enter my room in this way? You are only a guest in my father's house—that does not entitle you to force yourself on me.'

'Force! Now that's a strange word for you to use. If you were not waiting for me, then it must be your French lover, but you'll be disappointed. I saw him not ten minutes ago, with one of the maids. His taste in women leaves much to be desired.'

'As do your manners. If you do not leave this instant, I'll call for help,' Isabel said coldly.

An ugly scowl crossed James's face. He followed her as she moved away, caught her by the arm and pushed her back against a bedpost.

'I'm tired of your games, Madame la Marquise.'

'And I of you and your insufferable attitude. Think what you will of me, but keep it to yourself and leave me alone.' Isabel clutched nervously at the front of her bodice, which was in danger of falling to her waist. She probably did look as if she had been waiting for some-one, but it was none of his business, true or not. The way he was looking at her made her feel weak at the knees. His burning eyes never wavered from her flushed face and she had the feeling he could see into the very depths of her mind. Could he read how terrified she was of his embraces—his kisses—even the nearness of him? Oh God, she thought in silent agony—please make him go before it's too late!

James's fingers slid over the satin smoothness of her shoulders, then tightened around her arms, and she found herself being drawn against his chest, as helpless as a fly caught in a spider's web. She had no strength to resist the frightening hold this man held over her. No weapon except the acid tongue she had used to try and keep her own husband at bay. Flinging back her head, she stared up into the triumphant face above her, demanding:

'And why of all men, James MacLeod, should I take *you* to my bed?'

The contempt in her voice penetrated James's drink-hazed mind and momentarily sobered him. For a moment he stared at her in silence, then a soft chuckle rose in his throat and she knew her desperate gamble had not paid off. He was jealous of her. She had never experienced true jealousy in a man before and so did not know how to combat it. He believed her to be a whore and hated her for it, yet the sight of her with other men had brought him to her room seeking a terrible revenge.

How her husband Julian would have laughed to see her in such a situation. James would have been an ideal choice for his schemes and the one man Isabel could not have denied. She had fallen in love with him! Her eyes widened with the realisation, for with it came the knowledge she had to fight against his determination to master her or be destroyed by the only man who had ever meant anything to her. Once she belonged to him he would never believe her to be anything but what Malcolm proclaimed.

James gave a surprised oath as she raked at his cheeks with her nails, and the sudden pain unleashed the anger and disappointment he had been experiencing all evening.

His weight bore Isabel, struggling and sobbing, back on to the bed and held her helpless beneath him. Her clenched fists thudded into the side of his head as his fingers tugged at her bodice and pulled it and the shift beneath away from her breasts. The touch of his hands on her bare skin brought Isabel's resistance to an abrupt halt. She closed her eyes against the mocking face above her, biting her lips to stop herself crying out as the dark recesses of her mind opened to free unpleasant memories. She shivered, and out of the shadows above her James's voice said harshly:

'Whatever made you think you would take *me* to your bed? I warned you if you ever met a real man he would do the seeking and the taking. That's right, Isabel, close your eyes—pretend it's Jean-Paul or one of the many others who had your favours—I promise you, you won't be able to pretend for long.'

Isabel gave a choked-off cry and tried to turn away as his face loomed above hers, but he forced it back and began to kiss her with a fierceness that almost rendered her insensible. The room blurred and faded and was replaced by another. She could never escape that splendidly furnished room and the huge bed where she had endured so much suffering night after night as the old man at her side tried to prove he was not impotent as the court at Versailles liked to whisper behind his back. He would give her a child—she would produce his heir for them to see. Isabel moaned and fought against the suffocating embrace in which she was enfolded, but she was held fast and her strength was gone.

'My God, but you're a cold bitch.'

Startled, she opened her eyes upon the furious

features above her. She was not in Paris but in her own
room at Asher Mor, and it was not Julian who held her
but James MacLeod. He had mistaken the fear she had
been experiencing for coldness.

'Did you think you were the only man to try and force
his attentions on me?' Isabel mocked. How easy it was
to hurt him after the memories he had unwittingly
unleashed. 'You will have no better luck than they did.
Oh, yes—you are strong enough to take me by force, no
doubt you will be proud of such a victory. I won't stop
you—I can't, but I promise you, you'll gain no pleasure
from it.'

'Don't be too sure,' James warned and leaned
threateningly over her. His words seemingly had no
effect and he stopped, puzzled by her attitude. He was
not quite sure what he had expected when he entered
her room—or why he had come, apart from the fact he
had found himself outrageously jealous at the sight of
her dancing with so many other men. He had wanted to
see her—to talk perhaps or to hold her again and feel
the softness of her pressed against him. And he had
found her, so he thought, half undressed and waiting for
her lover. Why else had she not gone to bed? Who else
would go to her late at night but the Frenchman?

Isabel took advantage of his confusion.

'Why are you waiting, James? I'm only a helpless
woman. I shall endure you as I did my husband—he
never considered a woman's feelings either. I used to lie
awake at night steeling myself for the moment when he
climbed in beside me and touched me.'

A long shiver racked her body and James's hands
slowly fell away from her body. 'You and he have a
great deal in common. He was far older than you, of
course. Somehow you remind me of a little boy, James,
determined to have something you know is forbidden,
and you'll use any kind of deceit or trickery to have it.'

'That's enough.' James had drawn away from her to

the edge of the bed. She lay where he had left her, her eyes fastened on his face, cold, accusing.

'You and Malcolm will be able to laugh over this in the morning,' Isabel went on relentlessly, 'though he'll never understand why you didn't carry it through. No more do I. After all I'm just another whore, so why should I be treated with respect——' She broke off, the tears flooding down over her cheeks as reaction overcame her struggle for composure, and as if only then realising her state of undress, she clutched at her undershift in an attempt to cover herself and turned her face into the pillows, sobbing uncontrollably.

Was it her imagination or did she hear James's voice whisper unsteadily, 'Forgive me' and did she feel the gentle touch of his hand against her hair? Weakly she raised her head, but she was alone.

CHAPTER
FIVE

ISABEL opened her eyes on to a bedroom full of sunshine. The curtains had been drawn back from the windows and Simone was busy laying out her morning clothes. As she sat up, the maid turned and looked across at her and Isabel realised she had fallen asleep where she lay, still in her ball-gown and torn shift.

'It was him, wasn't it?'

Isabel got up and began to undress. The events of the night before seemed unreal—if she had not been in such a dishevelled state she might have thought it had all been a hideous nightmare.

'If you are referring to James MacLeod—yes, it was. He was drunk.'

Simone went into an explosion of French as she saw the dark smudges on her mistress's wrists and arms.

'I warned you he was dangerous, but you wouldn't listen. Jean-Paul will surely kill him.'

Pulling on a wrap, Isabel sat down before the dressing-table and held out a pair of silver-backed brushes.

'My hair is in a terrible mess, Simone, please do something with it at once.'

'*Mon Dieu*, have you taken leave of your senses? Did you not hear what I said?'

'I heard.'

'How are you so calm—so—so——'

'Indifferent is the word,' Isabel answered quietly. 'James acted no different from other men I have known—at least most of the time. But to put your mind at rest, we had an argument, nothing more. As for

Jean-Paul, you will say nothing of this to him unless you want me to send you back to France on the next boat.'

Through the glass, Isabel met Simone's disbelieving eyes.

'You are different this morning.' The maid stared at her, lost for words.

'Last night I learned I was capable of something other than hate.'

'Not—love! Not with him!'

'Why not with him?' Isabel stood up irritably. 'That's enough, I have a headache. I think I'll go riding.'

'Shall I tell Jean-Paul?' Simone asked pointedly.

'No, I prefer to go by myself. I have to think.'

'About how to avoid the man who loves you killing the man you say you love,' Simone retorted, and Isabel looked at her, aghast. If Jean-Paul learned of what had taken place there would surely be a fight.

'You must not tell him!'

'He is my brother, do you think I want to see him killed?' Simone demanded, then her fierce expression faded at the sight of the misery on Isabel's face. 'If you do love the MacLeod, you must follow the dictates of your heart. God knows you deserve some happiness. I pray he will be good to you.'

'I said I loved him—I did not say he loved me,' Isabel murmured. 'With what he believes, how could he ever have even one decent feeling for me? Come and help me to dress and forget I ever spoke of James MacLeod. Once Duncan is a free man again I can go back to the château—where I can find plenty of ways to forget him.'

Back to France, and the malicious tongues which had driven her almost into a life of seclusion? Even a life with the MacLeod would be preferable to that, Simone thought.

Outside her room Isabel encountered Lachlan, on his way to tell her she was wanted by her father. Alistair

was out of bed and sitting fully dressed in a chair beside
the fire. She was surprised he was even awake after such
a hectic evening, but pleased because his health seemed
to be improving. She bent and kissed his cheek and then
quickly drew back as a tall figure stepped away from the
windows and came to stand behind the chair.

'Good morning, Isabel.' James inclined his head
towards her. There was no smile on his dark features.
He seemed uneasy and would not meet her gaze. Was it
any wonder after his outrageous behaviour? she
thought bitterly.

'I will come back later when you are alone, Father.'

'No, Isabel—you will stay—James also. He has told
me what happened last night and apologised,' Alistair
answered, and his tone belied argument.

'I have heard no apology,' Isabel said stiffly.

'James will offer one to you in his own time.'

Isabel flashed a hostile look at the silent man. She
had forgotten how close he was to her father. Not for
one moment did she believe he had told the truth.

'He has asked for your hand in marriage,' Alistair
added. The shock of his words completely shattered
Isabel, and it was some considerable time before she
found herself saying:

'You forced me into a marriage once before,
Father—you promised never to interfere in my life
again.' Her face became an expressionless mask, and
she looked at the two men before her as if they were
strangers. Was she to be betrayed again? 'If my presence here distresses you I can always return to France.'

'You would never reach the boat, I'd see to that.'
James stepped towards her, but halted as she moved
back disdainfully. 'Listen to your father. Obey
him—and save yourself further unpleasantness. He has
agreed to the match.'

'Father, no—I will not marry him,' Isabel cried, her
hands clenching into tight fists at her sides. 'You have

no right. He should be down on his knees begging my forgiveness for what he did last night, not standing beside you like one of the family.'

'James has my permission to wed you, but only if you agree. If you do not, then it is up to you to discourage him—your experiences in France should have taught you how to do that.'

'Marriage to Julian taught me many things, Father.'

Isabel could hardly believe she had heard him speak such cruel words. So, after all, he did not believe in her innocence. 'What right have you to sit there and tell me again I must marry the man of your choice? Are you so desperate for a grandson? Julian married me to get an heir and you married Mary to Malcolm for the same reason. That's all you care about, isn't it? Not me—or Malcolm. None of your children are as important to you as a child to carry on your name. Well, I won't provide you with one—with James or any other man. I believed I was welcome here—that you wanted me at Asher Mor. But you've proved I am only here for one reason, to be pushed on to the first man who looks my way—to give you your precious heir.'

'No—no, child—I want only what is best for you.' Alistair stretched out a hand towards her, but she ignored it.

'I should have let Jean-Paul kill you,' she flung at James, and ran out of the room.

He and Alistair were engaged in a game of chess when they were interrupted by Simone in search of Isabel.

'She left me half an hour ago,' Alistair said, without looking up from the game.

'Was your mistress going out?' James asked curiously. 'I see you have her gloves and cloak.'

'Yes, monsieur, she was going riding.' Simone looked apprehensively at the rain pounding against the windows. 'But she would not go out in such weather unless——'

'Unless what, woman?' Alistair sat upright in his chair, obviously disturbed.

'Unless she was upset,' Simone answered reluctantly.

'She was,' James said shortly, 'but she grew up in this part of the country, you have no need to worry.'

'You are either a fool or a very heartless man not to care,' Simone replied stonily. 'I remember the last time she ran away. I will go after her myself.'

James's lips tightened. Twice in one hour he had been called that name. Three long strides brought him in front of Simone as she hurried to the door.

'Tell me about the last time,' he demanded.

Simone stared at him defiantly. She had promised never to speak of it to a living soul, but there was no way around his tall frame, and her mistress did profess to be in love with him. She had to risk trusting him—for Isabel's sake.

'Don't try my patience,' James warned, 'or I'll have your tongue loosened with a sound beating. Speak.'

'Madame tried to escape eight months after she was first married.'

'You talk in riddles. Escape from whom?'

'Her husband, the Marquis. Who else?' Simone replied, with a contemptuous twist of her narrow mouth. 'The inhuman monster hired two men—scum—to go after her. You should have seen how they brought her back, three days later, tied to the pommel of her horse like a runaway servant, half frozen and fainting from hunger.'

'What lies are you trying to make us believe? Why should the Marquis treat his wife in such a fashion?' James was clearly not convinced.

'Should you not be asking why Madame was so terrified that she ran away?' Simone countered.

'Very well, why did she?'

'You will have to ask her yourself, monsieur, I have

told you too much already,' the maid returned, and her face set into a determined expression which told James he would learn nothing more.

'I'll go after her,' he said to Alistair. 'I think I know where she will go.'

'I pray you do, monsieur,' Simone muttered. 'She will have need of someone. There was a storm that night, too . . .'

Fierce winds accompanied the storm that raged throughout the afternoon and villagers the length and breadth of the coast shut themselves in their crofts, built up their peat fires and looked out apprehensively at the black sky. The fisherfolk around Sandwood Bay barred their doors against the howling gale, muttering among themselves that D'hommil Dhu was walking the sands, along with the many poor souls whose ships had floundered on the dangerous rocks.

By late afternoon the winds slackened and a blanket of heavy mist settled over the wet heather.

Isabel had urged her horse away from Asher Mor at a gallop, careless of the rain which soaked her to the skin before she had crossed the courtyard. For hours she rode blindly, not seeing where she went, uncaring, so long as she was far away from James MacLeod. She was torn between the conflicting emotions of love and hate—both for the same man. She no more had a say in the final decision than if her father had ordered her to marry—James would see to that.

What would he do if she refused? she wondered, send men to steal her away to De'n Ceo or try to compromise her as he had the night before? She had no reputation to defend, but to save the honour of her father's name she would be forced to accept the marriage.

If she agreed of her own free will, it would not work either. Every time he held her in his arms he would wonder how many men before him had made love to her, and when she looked into his eyes she would for ever see the unasked questions. Most important of all there was Duncan to be considered, for she placed his happiness above her own. While he was dishonoured there could be no marriage for her and no happiness for either of them. The lives of three people thrown into disorder, and all due to Malcolm.

He had begun the vicious circle six years before, in Paris, when he had lost all his money at the gambling tables and Julian, Marquis de Riché, had had him thrown into the dreaded Bastille for non-payment of his debts. Isabel had been persuaded to seek an audience with the wealthy Marquis and plead with him to have her brother freed, not knowing Malcolm had already discussed her as a prospective candidate with the man he knew was seeking a young wife to give him an heir.

Isabel shivered as she recalled that first encounter with the man she was later to marry, but she was not allowed to dwell on it, for her horse, carefully picking its way over the waterlogged ground, suddenly shied as it stepped into a hole and she was thrown face down on to the heather. When she recovered her senses she found herself covered in mud and alone in the thickening mist.

She had been thrown before and was not unduly worried by it, but as she stood up and rubbed a bruised shoulder she realised she had completely lost all sense of direction. The enveloping mist made everything eerily silent—even the sound of the sea sounded far away.

If she could reach the edge of the cliffs and find a familiar landmark the rest would be comparatively easy, she thought, and began to trudge in what she hoped was the right direction, straining her ears for the guiding sound of the sea breaking on the shore.

She noticed it was growing darker and realised that it was nearly evening. Her father should have sent out a search party by now, though how they would ever find her when she could scarcely see one foot in front of the other she did not know. The rain slackened slightly, but her relief was short lived as a penetrating wind blew up, chilling her to the bone. She was seized with bouts of shivering, but dared not rest for fear she should become so cold she could not go on.

She did not see the horseman until he loomed up only feet in front of her, but she heard the loud oath as she threw herself sideways to avoid a headlong collision, and as she lay dazed and half fainting strong hands caught her by the shoulders and turned her over.

'Isabel—are you hurt? Where's your horse?'

She stared unbelievingly into the dark face above her. James MacLeod—of all men, he had to find her. He was soaking wet, too, and the rain was dripping from his black hair on to her cheeks. She ran a shaky hand across her eyes to brush away the loose hair plastered there.

'I was thrown, but I'm all right.' She ached in every limb, but was determined he would never know it. 'Where are the others?'

'What others?' James looked at her blankly.

'You—you came to look for me alone?' She struggled to sit up, biting her lips as a violent pain seared her back. It had been hurting ever since her fall.

James helped her, with a humourless smile.

'I guessed where you would be, but I didn't expect to find you in such a sorry state.' He swung about suddenly, cursing as he remembered he had not bothered to tether his horse. It was gone, and with it their only chance of safely reaching Asher Mor. 'Devil take the animal! We shall have to find a place to stay until the mist clears.'

'I don't even know where we are,' Isabel said lamely.

'Above Sandwood. You were heading towards the cliffs. You could have fallen.'

'The sound of the sea was guiding me.'

'To your death! Give me your hand, we're almost to

the path. There's an old croft halfway down where we can shelter and get a fire going to dry those clothes of yours before you catch a chill.'

Without waiting for an answer, he took her tightly by the hand and drew her to her feet. Isabel looked at him searchingly as he pulled her jacket more closely around her, but his touch was impersonal and there was no expression on his face to tell her his thoughts.

Wordlessly she allowed him to lead her, still unable to believe he was really with her. Had her father asked him to follow her or had it been his own idea? No, it could not be, she decided, for it would mean deep down inside him there was a spark of feeling for her, and that was not possible.

She stumbled and almost fell on the uneven ground. Her legs were beginning to grow horribly weak and her steps faltered. James swung round in time to catch her as she reeled unsteadily.

'You little fool, whatever possessed you to ride out in such a storm?'

'I wanted to get away.' The last of Isabel's defiance blazed at him from her tawny eyes with the answer.

'From me?'

'Yes.'

'That you will never do. You and I belong together. If you ever leave me I'll follow you wherever you go and bring you back,' James said in a calm tone that completely robbed her of all speech.

As easily as if she was a child, he lifted her up in his arms and continued on down the path to the ruined croft just visible before them. Shouldering open the door, he carried her inside, kicked it shut and set her down with a curt, 'Stay put while I find a torch.'

Isabel leaned back against the wall without whose support she would have been unable to stand, and listened to him moving about in the darkness, swearing as he stumbled and had to kick things from his path. A

moment later a torch flared to life. Without looking at
her, James thrust it into the earth, wedged it firmly
between two stones and began gathering together the
pieces of wood strewn everywhere.

Thank goodness the roof was in one piece, Isabel
thought, trying to hide her dismay as she stared at their
dismal surroundings. All the roughly made furniture
had been broken and there was nowhere to sit down let
alone make a bed. Probably the previous occupant had
been frightened away by tales of the ghostly figures
walking the sands of Sandwood. Nothing, not even a
ghost, would induce her to leave the protective shelter
the croft offered.

As a fire blazed into life, James stood up, muttering,
'Thank God the wood was dry. Come here where it's
warm and take off those wet clothes.'

He had stripped off his sodden coat and shirt and
spread them out on the ground before realising she had
not moved. Removing his sword and the dirk, he wiped
them carefully on his plaid and put them to one side,
then came across to her, caught her by the arm and
dragged her unceremoniously to the fire.

'I'm in no mood for games, girl. Do as I tell you or I'll
undress you myself,' he thundered.

Hugging her arms about her, Isabel sank down on
her knees before the fire. James knelt beside her and
was unfastening her jacket before she realised what he
was doing. With a cry she pushed his hands away.

'Leave me alone.'

'You are mighty particular who touches you these
days,' James said cruelly, and proceeded to pull off the
coat despite her protests. His fingers reached out
towards the buttons of her blouse, the look on his face
warning her that he intended to carry out his threat.

'If you struggle I'll knock you cold,' he growled. 'I
don't want a sick girl on my hands in the morning—
I'll have some explaining to do to Alistair as it is. It

will be easier for everyone if you agree to my marriage offer.'

'To save my honour after being alone here with you all night?' Isabel gave a brittle laugh that bordered on hysteria. Looking at her, James saw there was not a trace of colour in her ashen cheeks, but her eyes looked bright with fever and her skin was beginning to burn beneath his hands. He did not rise to the taunt and went on with his task. Isabel sat shivering as he spread her outer clothes near the flames, forcing back the tears which threatened to come and praying he would not touch her. Every time he looked at her she remembered how good it felt to have his arms around her, and was bitterly ashamed.

'They shouldn't take too long to dry,' James declared, standing over her. What a pathetic picture she made in only a wet shift, her loose hair clinging limply to her face and shoulders, yet despite her dejected appearance he was acutely aware of the woman and how fiercely he wanted her. Isabel flinched away as he reached down and stroked the fair hair away from her face.

'You'll have to get used to my touch, Isabel—and much more,' he said quietly.

'When, James? Now? Are you going to make sure I have no choice in the matter? It shouldn't be difficult for you after last night.'

'That was a mistake. I was drunk, but I knew what I was doing. If I hadn't I'd have taken you.'

Isabel looked away from his burning eyes, knowing he spoke the truth. As a spasm of shivering seized her, James sat down at her side and pulled her close against him, ignoring her weak protests. Unwillingly Isabel submitted to the hard contact of his body against hers and allowed him to try to rub some warmth back into her frozen limbs.

'Don't fight me, girl—you know you don't want to.'

She turned her face against a firm, damp shoulder and tried to ignore the touch of his mouth against her hair.

'Do what you like with me—you have the strength—but I'll never marry you.' She tried to sound unconcerned but failed miserably.

'When I saw you again at Scourie I liked what I saw and I wanted you. I'm a man used to taking what he wants—and I will, but in my own time.'

Isabel snatched herself free of his grasp and withdrew to the far side of the fire. James stood up and went to the window, hardening his heart against the appeal in her eyes. He allowed his eyes to wander insultingly over the clinging shift before answering her unasked question.

'No—I'm not going to make love to you, there's no need for it. When I say you belong only to me, you know it's the truth; I don't have to prove it.'

'I will never belong to you. You will own only my body.' Isabel swayed, seized with sudden fatigue, but the moment James started towards her she drew herself upright and said coldly:

'I am all right. Leave me to rest.'

Crouching beside the fire, James picked up his jacket and held it out towards the crackling flames. Without looking at her he demanded:

'Why did you run away from your husband?'

'Simone!' Isabel breathed. She could hardly believe her maid had broken a confidence, but there was no one else apart from Jean-Paul.

'She wanted to avoid a beating. You haven't answered my question.'

'You have no right to bully my servants, and less to pry into my personal life.'

'I shall pry as much as I please. A sound whipping might not do you any harm—it could even make you more obedient.' James scowled across at her in such a

fashion that she could well believe had he had a whip at
hand he would have used it on her. 'I'm not one of your
fawning courtiers, Isabel. Either you give me an answer
or I'll come over there and shake it out of you.'

'What is it you want to know?' Isabel knew he would
never believe her after listening to Malcolm's lies, but
she could not lose the chance of telling him the truth.

'Your maid said you ran away. Why?'

'Because I couldn't stand him any longer.'

'By him, do you mean your husband?'

She nodded mutely.

'After eight months of marriage you grew tired of
him. Where were you going—to Paris—to the bed of a
younger man—a lover, perhaps?'

Isabel's lips quivered at his callousness. Locking her
hands tightly in her lap she stared into his face proudly.

'After eight months of being used by an old man to
try and have an heir, I was blamed because there was
no child. He had endless doctors to examine me, but
they all pronounced me fit. That day one of them told
him the fault was not mine, but his. He flew into a rage
and had me locked in my room for two days without
food or drink. When he came to me again it was the
same as always, and he realised finally the doctor had
spoken the truth. He cried on my breast like a little boy,
caressing me until I felt sick, begging me to take a lover
and give him an heir.' She heard James's sharp intake
of breath and stopped before she had said she did not
agree.

'And you were only too willing to agree. The longer
you delayed having a child, the more men to dance
attendance on you.'

'If I say that is a lie, will you believe me?'

Her question was met with a humourless smile and
she shrugged her slim shoulders. 'Then I will not deny
it. Did Malcolm also tell you why Father agreed to my
marriage to Julian?'

'He spoke of a debt of honour.' James did not bother to deny that he and Malcolm had discussed her past.

'Honour!' Her voice was bitter. 'Malcolm has no conception of the word. We were staying in France with my mother's family. His manners were atrocious. He shamed them wherever he went, drank heavily and gambled away all his money, including that he got from the sale of my jewellery which he stole from my room. When he lost at the tables and the winners wanted to be paid, he would insult them, sometimes challenge them to a duel. Few of them were ever paid or took up his challenges—until he met Julian. When Malcolm failed to meet his obligations he was thrown into the Bastille.'

She paused and looked enquiringly at James, who stood silent, watchful, his arms folded across his bare chest. 'Shall I go on?'

'Why not? Confession is good for the soul, isn't it?'

'On Malcolm's behalf I went to see Julian,' she continued. 'A week later he came here to Asher Mor to tell my father that Malcolm would be released as soon as he agreed to my marrying Julian. Within the month I was married. On my wedding day Malcolm told me that he had told Julian I would make him a good wife—bear him many children—he arranged everything before Julian ever left France. Father's consent was a mere formality. My worth was no more than the amount of the gambling debts. I was seventeen and Julian was fifty-nine,' she added in an effort to show him how impossible life had been for her.

James's face was dark with anger and there was a dangerous gleam in his eyes, and for a moment she expected a word of sympathy. Reaching down for his coat, he tossed it across to her, saying curtly:

'It's almost dry. Put it around you and go to sleep. As soon as it's morning I'll try to find the horses.'

Isabel wrapped it around her and lay down, her back towards him. She ached in every limb and her back made it impossible to be comfortable, but exhaustion overcame her and she soon fell asleep.

James slept, awakening as the cold, grey light of dawn was lighting the sky outside, with the knowledge they were no longer alone in the croft. Through half-closed eyes he could make out four or five shadowy figures moving about near the dying embers of the fire. Rolling away from Isabel he made a desperate bid for his sword, but a savage blow on the back of the head sent him sprawling into the dirt. He heard Isabel scream as he pulled himself, reeling, on to his knees, saw her throw herself at the man whose swordpoint was aimed at his chest and stay the thrust.

'No, Duncan, no! Spare him.'

'Get away from me, you whore!' Duncan spun round on her with an oath, and the flat of his hand caught her across both cheeks. 'You are all they said you were—you are no sister of mine. From this moment I have no kin.'

James's mouth twisted into an angry snarl at the sight of the blood at the corner of Isabel's mouth, but the effort proved too much for him and he slumped unconscious to the floor.

'He'll be quiet for a while,' Duncan muttered with a satisfied smile. Isabel's tears dissolved in amazement as he took her in his arms and hugged her. 'Has he hurt you?'

Wordlessly she shook her head. Gently he wiped away the thin trickle of blood at the corner of her mouth.

'I'm sorry for such rough treatment, little one, but if you want him to live, he must not know you are helping me. I've been told you are in love with him, though I don't believe it.'

'Duncan—wait, my head is reeling. I wake up to find you here accusing me of all manner of things, then you hit me and say I am no longer your sister. Now you say

James's life will be spared because I love him. Who told you such a thing? How did you find us?'

'I was planning to leave for Inverness this morning when *en route* my men and I found two riderless horses. We started a search at once and then we met your maid. She told us of the quarrel you had with James——'

'It was more with Father. James wants to marry me and he agreed.'

'The devil he did! No wonder you left the house in a state.'

'My reasons were very personal, but they don't matter now,' Isabel said quietly. 'Are my clothes dry, Duncan? Despite my reputation I prefer to be fully dressed.'

He handed them to her with a searching look.

'James came after you alone?'

'Yes—when he found me I was on foot and exhausted. The mist was too thick to go on, so we found shelter here. I give you my word he has not harmed me. On the contrary, he seems determined to keep his distance until we are married. After what has happened now, I have no choice.'

'You can go to Inverness with me—James won't follow, I promise you.'

'He's sworn to come after me wherever I go, and I believe him. Both of us know he doesn't make promises he won't keep. If Simone told you I love him, it's the truth. I never intended him to find out, and as for wanting to marry me'—Isabel shook her head helplessly. 'I don't know his reasons—only that it must be.'

'You are a rich widow and James still owes Father money from the last rising,' Duncan muttered, with a sidelong glance at the unconscious man. 'Have you not thought of that?'

'No, I had not,' Isabel admitted, 'but it makes little difference.'

'Then you do not need my help.' Duncan took her

firmly by the shoulders and made her look at him. 'I
shall be in Inverness if you come to your senses—send
for me or come and I'll protect you. You may love
James now, but he could kill everything you feel for him
if he discovers why you came back to Scotland. It would
save us both a great deal of trouble if you'd let me
dispose of him now.'

'I love James as deeply—as sincerely as you loved
Kirsty Fraser,' Isabel said slowly, and Duncan released
her with a faint smile.

'Then I'll not argue with you any longer. Do you
think I've convinced him we are no longer friends?'

'I think so—let me worry about it. Go now before it
grows any lighter and you are seen.'

From the doorway of the croft, Isabel watched Duncan and his men clamber up the path to where their
horses were tethered and guarded by one man. They
rode off, leaving behind her own mount and James's
stallion. He was beginning to recover as she returned to
his side and she bent to gather up his sword and dirk as
he rolled over dazedly, clutching his head.

'Isabel!' He stared at her stupidly for a moment,
then, as his memory flooded back, he swayed to his feet
and lurched across to the door. 'Where are they?'

'Gone.'

'Leaving me alive?' He wheeled on her, his eyes dark
with suspicion. 'You saved me from Duncan's
sword—why? He could have prevented a marriage you
obviously have no taste for.'

'That was my mistake.' She chose her words carefully, deliberately continuing the pretence Duncan had
begun. 'Because of it he believes we are lovers and I
have lost a brother.'

'A man who has no trust in his own flesh and blood is
of little consequence.' He came across to her and lightly
touched her bruised mouth with fingers so gentle the
tears started to Isabel's eyes. 'Can you still believe he

did not murder Kirsty? He is a man of moods no less
than Malcolm. Perhaps in his way he did love her, but
in a jealous rage he killed her. In jealousy he struck you
and disowned you because he found you here with me.
So little trust for one who loved him so much.'

'Take me home, please, James.' Isabel turned
quickly away to hide her confusion. 'Duncan has left
our horses at the top of the cliff.'

'How generous—but at least it saves us walking back
to Asher Mor, so I'll not grumble.'

Isabel almost ran out of the croft. The bright sunlight
outside was dazzling after the murky mists of the
previous evening. They rode side by side in
silence—following the line of the cliffs homewards until
James suddenly reined in, staring across the water to
where De'n Ceo was clearly visible in the early morning
sunshine.

'If I were to take you there now, Isabel, it would not
be against your will and we both know it. Soon—very
soon—there will be no pretence between us.' He broke
off, staring ahead through narrowed eyes to the group
of riders fast approaching them. His hand fell to his
sword and he ordered curtly, 'Stay close—they could
be Duncan's men. We could have walked into a pretty
trap——'

'No—look! They are MacLeods from Asher
Mor—and Jean-Paul.'

The Frenchman was riding out in front of the others
and was the first to reach them. Isabel marvelled at his
self-control as he acknowledged her—and the man at
her side—without an angry sign. Whatever he thought
of her spending the night on the moors with James, she
knew she would never know.

'Madame, you are needed at Asher Mor—hurry.
'Tis your father,' he muttered. 'When you did not
return he collapsed late last night.'

Isabel cast a despairing glance into James's

sympathetic face. Was her happiness to be threatened by yet another tragedy—a tragedy this time of her own making? If she had not run away——

Asher Mor was an uneasily quiet house. Servants went about their business on tiptoe lest the slightest sound disturbed their sick chieftain.

Isabel was shocked at the deterioration in the man who lay still and silent in the bed before her. The face was lost of all colour—waxen—unreal, as if he was already dead. She reached out a trembling finger and touched the outstretched hand on the cover. Her father neither moved nor opened his eyes, but the gnarled fingers closed around her in a tight grip as if to ask her not to leave.

'All he wanted was for ye to come home and be with him.' Lachlan was beside her and there were tears in the old retainer's eyes.

'Why didn't he tell me he was so ill?' Isabel whispered. 'At the ball he was almost like his old self.'

'The effort cost him dear as you can see, mistress. He should have died months ago, but he held on like the stubborn old war-horse he is to see you again. Best come away and leave him, he doesn't know you are here.'

'He knows,' Isabel whispered, looking at the hand clasping hers. 'He knows.'

Isabel lost track of how long she remained beside her father. Time was not important. She sat by the bed oblivious to who came and went from the sick-room, ignoring the pleas of Lachlan and Simone to rest in her own room. Mary came and sat with her for a while, but did not remain long. Isabel thought she looked ill at ease and forgave her when she left—he was not her father. Malcolm did not put in an appearance at all. He would be downstairs drinking, she thought, awaiting the moment when he became head of the house. With the death of their father she would be at his mercy—all his suspicions would begin again and he would set men to watch her.

'Isabel—my child.' Alistair's eyes were open, fixed on his daughter's face. His voice was low and trembling. 'You—you came back.'

'James found me, Father, but we lost our horses and had to wait until the mists cleared. I'm quite safe now. Please don't worry—I won't leave you again, I promise.'

'No—it is I who am leaving you, and before I do I must know you will be protected—we both know from whom. Malcolm will try to destroy you as he did once before. I was too blind to see him for what he was then. I allowed you to become a pawn in a disastrous marriage. Whatever you did—and I by no means believe the gutter talk I have heard—I would not blame you. I must die knowing the same thing cannot happen again. Malcolm lusts after your money—to gain control of it he would devise the most devious of plans. If only Duncan was here to protect you.' He broke off, fighting for breath, but waved aside Isabel's plea to rest.

'Promise me you will marry James. Give him a chance and he will make you happy. He has his faults like any other man, and your money will do much for De'n Ceo and the village, but he will protect you with his life. You are well matched, Isabel!'

She raised her head and stared into her father's pain-ravaged features. Life was ebbing slowly from his tired body. Death would release him from illness and worry.

'I will do as you wish. I swear it.'

There was no answer. Gently disengaging her hand she stood up, not knowing if he heard her. A shadow fell across the bed and a comforting arm went around her drooping shoulders.

'Come and rest,' James whispered.

CHAPTER
SIX

'COME and rest, you've been sitting by your father's bedside for nearly nine hours without a break.' Ignoring Isabel's protests, James led her to her own room and sat her down in a chair before the fire. Simone followed them into the room, apprehensively eyeing first her mistress's pale face and then her dishevelled appearance, for Isabel was still wearing her creased riding habit and the blouse was streaked with mud. 'Don't stand there staring, woman, go and fetch your mistress some food and a hot drink.'

As the door closed behind her, Isabel rose to her feet and went into the bedroom. When she came out again she wore a pale-coloured wrap trimmed with fur and her tangled hair had been brushed back and secured at the nape of her neck by a comb. Silently James congratulated her on her self-control; it was magnificent.

'He's going to die, isn't he?' Her tone defied a lie and he nodded.

'It will be a blessed relief.'

'I know, but that doesn't make it easier to bear. I've so much to atone for, but no time.' Isabel sat down again with a deep sigh. 'You overheard, didn't you?'

'Yes.'

'I promised him I'll marry you and I will. I ask only that you be patient with me.'

James leaned against the mantel, staring down into the flames crackling at his feet.

'Your promise made him happy. I release you from it—I'll have you of your own free will or not at all.'

'On the way home you said if you took me to De'n

Ceo I would be willing, and you were right,' Isabel murmured. She forced herself to hold his gaze and meet the disbelief in his pale eyes. Now she had committed herself there was no need to lie or conceal her feelings any longer. He leaned forward as if to catch hold of her, and she immediately drew back. 'No, James, please don't touch me—I cannot think straight when you do. I will marry you—not just because of my promise to father, but for a reason you may not believe. I love you. I have never been in love before. When I am with you I'm afraid—of you, of your nearness—your touch. I have no defence against the way you make me feel.'

James's lips effectively silenced her. He lifted her out of the chair and held her against him in an embrace so tight she could scarcely breathe, but she was too happy to care. She clung to him, whispering his name, answering kiss for kiss until her head swam and she leaned against him weak and spent.

'James! James!'

'Say it again.'

'I love you. I have never loved another man. Do you believe me?'

'Looking at you—holding you—how can I not believe you?' James said hoarsely. He kissed her eager mouth and then her neck and felt her tremble.

'I will not treat you like all the others and I will not touch you until we are married. Alistair was right, we are well matched. You will see.'

'And my past?' Isabel faltered, lifting her head to look at him.

'Is forgiven, although one day, many years ahead, I'll ask you to tell me how you earned such a scandalous reputation—I have doubts as to its authenticity.'

'Let me tell you now,' she pleaded. 'There must be no secrets between us—nothing to make you look at me with a question in your eyes.'

James laid a hand across her mouth.

'Once we are married no man will dare mention what happened in France, and we will be far too busy to dwell on it.' James held her at arm's length, staring down into her flushed face with searching eyes. 'We both knew what would happen that first night you came back to Asher Mor, do you remember?'

Her first night at home when James had sat across the table from her at dinner and taunted her cruelly. 'You have yet to meet a real man. He will do the taking and you will have no say in the matter.' He had known better than she where her destiny lay.

'I don't deny I've had women,' James confessed. 'They made pleasant an otherwise dull existence, but I've never pretended to love any of them and they knew it. If you had not come back——' He broke off, his eyes narrowing sharply. 'It's taken me a long time to accept the way I feel about you.'

'Because of what I am?'

'What you were is in the past. You've known other men, but all that is over now. If you invite another man to touch you by so much as a smile, I'll kill him and you too. Jealousy is something else I've never known. I don't like the feeling or the knowledge of what I'm capable of doing if you ever betrayed me. Perhaps I love you too much.'

'Oh, James.' Isabel caught his face between her hands and kissed him as she had never kissed any other man before. For a moment James was still, then his arms enfolded her and she felt the depth of his feelings as he answered her.

For a long while he held her in silence, his lips pressed against her loose hair, then gently he put her from him and said goodnight.

Simone eyed the empty plate and glass on the tray beside her mistress's chair and gave a satisfied smile.

'Madame is looking much better.'

'Thank you, Simone, I feel it. Is there any change in my father?'

'Not yet. I spoke to Lachlan on my way back from the kitchen. He still sleeps. Why don't you try to rest too?'

'I think I will—I hardly slept at all last night, and don't look at me with such reproving eyes, James didn't make love to me. If you thought he meant to harm me, why did you tell him about the time I ran away from Julian?'

'I had to trust him—there was no one else. Did I do wrong?'

'If he hadn't come after me I'd never have known he loved me,' Isabel breathed. 'Oh, Simone, I have never been so happy. He treats me as if I am a queen.'

'Which is the way it should be. Go to bed now, *mignonne*, and dream of the future with your James.'

'I have no need to dream any longer, Simone, I have everything I want in this world.'

Simone turned down the bed and helped Isabel into her nightgown. As she blew out the candles both women heard the sound of shouting from somewhere below.

'That will be your brother,' the maid remarked. 'He's been in a bad mood all day.'

'And drinking, I suppose?' Isabel shivered as she recalled how mean Malcolm could be when his temper was inflamed by raw liquor.

'Since last night. The servants are afraid to go near him. His wife is at her wits' end. He abused her before all the servants, which is nothing unusual from what I hear—and the poor thing ran upstairs. Then he even turned on his steward.'

'Did he now? Isabel sat up, her expression growing thoughtful. 'How serious was their quarrel, do you know?'

'Your   brother   struck   him   during   a   violent

argument—none of the other servants seem to know what it was about, but one of the kitchen maids swears she heard the name Duncan mentioned. Perhaps the thieves are falling out.'

'Murderers, not thieves,' Isabel said quietly. 'I pray you are right. This may be the moment I've been waiting for. Malcolm has frightened everyone into holding their tongues about what really happened to James's ward, but now he has provided us with a weak link—Andrew Beaton. Lachlan tells me he is a vain man, greedy and ambitious. Blows and abuse are not the rewards he has expected for his part in the sordid affair. Tomorrow morning have Jean-Paul bring him to me.'

'What will you do? Bribe him? Have him beaten?'

'I don't know,' Isabel confessed, 'but I must do something. James has offered me his love and a new life—but I can have neither while he hunts Duncan.'

'Then give the steward to Jean-Paul,' Simone pleaded. 'You must. I won't let you throw away this chance of happiness.'

'If all else fails, I will. Let us wait and see what happens tomorrow.'

Andrew Beaton was in his late forties—a thick-set, stocky man, with receding hair and a sallow complexion. His father had served the laird before him, schooling his son to follow him, but Andrew had been passed over for the older, more experienced Lachlan and had become Malcolm's steward. His master's wild ways were a source of constant irritation to him; he was treated worse than the lowest servant in the household, sworn at, humiliated, for ever reminded he was only a servant with no rights or privileges. Servant! That would not last much longer. Once the old laird was dead and Malcolm ruled Asher Mor he would be rewarded for all his years of uncomplaining toil—and for keeping his master's unpleasant secret. He had been promised money and Lachlan's position in the house, more power than he had ever dreamed of.

He stood in Isabel's drawing-room, his eyes fastened on the array of jewels spread out on the table before him. Isabel was seated on the couch, examining the many pieces, occasionally handing something to Jean-Paul who sat at her side.

'Take these earrings too—and there is a stone missing from this necklace, it will have to be repaired.'

With a nod the Frenchman took the pieces and dropped them into the suède bag he held.

'And you may as well have this, Jean-Paul, you've always liked it.'

Andrew could scarcely keep the greed from his eyes as Isabel passed over a heavy gold ring set with rubies and diamonds, and Jean-Paul slipped it on to the little finger of his right hand.

'There—that's the last of them.' Isabel looked up at the man before her as if only then remembering his presence. 'Well—what is your answer?'

'Your offer is too kind, milady, but I am already bound to the Lord Malcolm.'

'Nonsense—what can he do if you choose to leave him, beat you? He does that anyway, so I've heard—and more. My brother is an egotistical bully, Andrew Beaton, with no respect for man or beast. When my servants serve me well they are rewarded.'

She glanced significantly at the ring on Jean-Paul's hand and saw the steward's eyes follow hers. She was taking a desperate chance in approaching him so boldly, but James had left her no choice. Before their wedding day, Duncan's innocence had to be proved—or disaster would surely overtake them before they had left the kirk.

'I do not intend to remain here much longer. Should my father get well, I shall leave within the month. If his health deteriorates ... I shall not remain beneath this roof when my brother becomes the laird. I have heard good reports of you, that is why I have offered you this chance to enter my service. You would not find me ungrateful for faithful service.'

'You misunderstood me, milady—I was—I was not refusing your generous offer.' Andrew Beaton's greedy nature had been aroused by the array of wealth before him. The ring on Jean-Paul's hand mocked him. Never in all his years of service with Malcolm had he been given any kind of remuneration—not even a kind word, only promises. What if they were not kept when the laird died? If he accepted this generous offer it was possible he would end up with his throat slit. Either way that threat hung over his head—dead men could not reveal secrets. 'Lord Malcolm would never allow me to leave his service.'

'Then you would consider it?'

The steward shrugged, but it was easy to see he was gradually weakening. 'Yes—why not? Milady has made her service appear most attractive.'

'And lucrative for the right man,' Isabel said meaningly. 'Malcolm need present no problem to us—we merely play by his set of dirty rules. What unpleasant secrets of his have you learned over the years? Once I have possession of something to use against him, you have nothing to worry about.'

At the word *secret*, Andrew Beaton's sallow complexion took on an ashen tinge. Jean-Paul rose to pour himself a glass of wine. He did not return to his seat but leaned idly against the chaise-longue, barring the way to the door. The steward's eyes narrowed as he stared at him, then at the woman on the couch. All his instincts warned him something was wrong, but he could not think what it was as yet. And then, looking into Isabel's hard eyes, he realised the trap which was closing relentlessly around him.

'Secrets, milady? There are no secrets at Asher Mor that you don't know about.'

'I think there is one. Come now, don't play games with me any longer. I had hoped to provide you with sufficient encouragement to loosen your tongue, but if you intend to be stubborn, we will have to resort to other methods. Tell me how Kirsty Fraser really died, Andrew Beaton, or I shall give you to Jean-Paul, who will have the information out of you in less than two hours. He knows of tortures far more subtle than those our countrymen use.'

The steward licked his lips nervously. His master's vengeance if he switched allegiances would be nothing compared to the terrible revenge he would inflict for divulging the secret of Kirsty Fraser's death and the events leading up to the night she died.

'If you talk now, my friend, you will save yourself a great deal of pain.' Jean-Paul straightened his hand on his sword. He stepped closer to Andrew Beaton and he was no longer smiling. 'Talk, you misbegotten fool, or I'll give you a taste of my fist.'

'Patience, Jean-Paul, you shall have him soon enough if he continues to remain silent.'

'I have nothing to say.' Andrew Beaton's mouth closed in a tight determined line.

Isabel rose to her feet. She was suddenly very pale. She had come to a crossroads. Her bluff had failed and the steward now knew why she had returned to Asher Mor. If she let him go he would report to Malcolm and then not only her mission but her very life would be in danger.

Jean-Paul made the decision for her. Stepping forward he struck the man on the back of the head with the butt of the pistol he had taken from inside his jacket.

'Simone, fetch me something to tie him with—the curtain cord will do.'

Isabel stood a silent observer as Simone did as she

was bid. She helped her brother securely tie the unconscious man and gag him, and then they rolled him in a
large rug which Jean-Paul dragged out from the bedroom.

'I took the precaution of having everything ready in
case he became difficult,' he said, smiling into her
questioning gaze. Without any effort he hoisted the
innocent-looking bundle over his shoulder. 'Should we
be seen there will be no awkward questions. Will you
show me a safe place to put him—somewhere where I
can question him undisturbed? I'm trying to make
things easy for you, *ma petite*,' he added when Isabel did
not move.

'I know and I'm grateful, but—I've never condemned a man to death before.'

'He can easily save his skin—he has only to tell us
what we want to know. Which life is more important—this man's or that of your brother, perhaps your
own?'

'You are right, of course,' Isabel sighed. 'Simone,
make sure no one is outside. We will take the back
staircase. Is it clear? Good! Let us go then—I feel as if a
hundred eyes are watching us.'

At the bottom of the narrow, dark staircase Isabel
stopped and took down a wall torch which Simone
lighted for her. Ahead of them stretched a winding
tunnel, the walls wet with green slime and dripping
with water.

'This leads under the moat,' Isabel said. 'The place
we want is at the end of this passage.'

Picking up her skirts she led the way. With an
apprehensive look at her brother Simone followed.
Several minutes later they came upon a large, heavily-
hinged door set in the rock. Handing the torch to her
maid, Isabel proceeded to pull back all the bolts. The
door was rusty with lack of use, and eventually Jean-

Paul put down his burden to help the two women drag it open.

Carefully Isabel picked her way down the flight of wet stone stairs to the sandy floor. They were standing in a large cave, the first of many, Jean-Paul realised as he looked around. From all sides led off small passageways, probably leading to other caves.

'This used to be a smuggler's paradise,' Isabel said. 'At high tide a small boat can come in here and the contraband unloaded and stored away in a dry place until it could be moved.' She pointed ahead to where a shaft of sunlight struck the bare rocks in front of them. 'The entrance is not far ahead—the water floods this cave completely, almost to the door. You will have to find a safe place to put our guest, we don't want him accidentally drowned. Be careful of the tide yourself, it comes in with horrifying speed—and be sure to bolt the door when you leave. No one usually comes down here, but if they do they must find nothing to make them suspicious.'

Jean-Paul looked around him and nodded in satisfaction. This was an ideal place to work.

'Take yourselves out of here, this is no place for women,' he said, bending to release his prisoner from the encumbrance of the rug.

Simone took Isabel's arm with a look that warned her not to argue. Isabel hurried up the stairs without a backward glance, sensing that the violence she had always known existed in Jean-Paul was about to be unleashed.

Isabel bathed and changed into one of her Paris gowns, expectantly awaiting James's arrival, but as the sky darkened outside her window she realised he was not coming. Simone came in to find her mistress anxiously pacing the room.

'What is it?' she exclaimed.

'Something is wrong—it must be, or he would have come. Why hasn't he come, Simone?'

Simone took her by the hand and pushed her gently but firmly into a chair.

'*Mon Dieu*, you are like a young girl in love for the first time,' she laughed, then her mockery faded as she saw the flush of colour rising in Isabel's cheeks. 'Forgive me, *mignonne*, I have a thoughtless tongue. The MacLeod is your first love—and he is also a man of unpredictable moods. You will never rule him and so you must learn to expect him only when you see him. But he is also a considerate man, he obviously knew you would be waiting and he has sent his steward with a message—and a gift,' she added.

'Show him in quickly, before I die of curiosity,' Isabel cried, her agitation fading.

Simone ushered in Bran MacKay. He carried something wrapped in a piece of cloth and a letter. Conscious of his eyes on her and trying hard to conceal her rising excitement, Isabel broke the seal and read it.

In a large, bold hand James had written: 'May the gift I send you—my future wife, mistress of De'n Ceo—protect you as successfully as other members of my family. I shall ride over to see you tomorrow.'

'Please!' Isabel stretched out her hands for the carefully wrapped present. She knew what it was before her trembling fingers touched the softness of the 'Green Mantle'.

'My master has honoured you,' Bran MacKay exclaimed. By the astonishment on his face it was obvious he had not known what he was carrying.

'I am aware of it,' Isabel returned quietly. 'I thank you for bringing me such a wonderful gift.'

'Do you have a message for my master?' Bran looked at her curiously. She looked somehow different from when he had seen her before—not only her appearance. There was a warmth radiating from her—and the pale amber eyes were no longer cold but shining with happiness. Had James MacLeod brought about this transformation?

'Tell him——' Isabel broke off, a faint tinge of pink creeping into her cheeks, 'tell him I shall be waiting for him.'

Bran MacKay bowed and left her.

She was seated in her drawing-room trying to concentrate on a piece of embroidery when James rode into the courtyard and immediately she threw it aside and ran into the bedroom to inspect her appearance. Her dress was of dark blue velvet, cut low across her breasts and away from the shoulders. A fichu of white lace covered the latter and the same material was set into the slashed sleeves. A heavy necklace of sapphires adorned her throat and a pair of matching earrings hung from her ears. Simone had spent hours brushing her hair and had arranged it in a thick coil at the base of her neck, tied with a dark blue bow. She looked flushed, over-eager to see him, Isabel thought, and yet where was the shame in that?

When Simone showed him into her presence and discreetly withdrew, Isabel stood trembling before him, her breath catching in her throat at the expression which rose in his face as his eyes swept over her.

'My darling—you look lovely,' James said and swept her into his arms. The kisses Isabel had dreamed of only a few short hours before lifted her to dizzy heights and she clung to him near to tears.

'You didn't believe I'd come.' James stared down at her, amazed by the bright flood brimming in her eyes.

'So much has happened these past few days I'm not sure of anything,' Isabel whispered, 'only that I love you.'

'And that I love you.' James caught her chin in firm fingers and held it fast. His pale eyes glittered with wicked lights as he lowered his mouth to hers and continued to kiss her until he was sure she was convinced.

She gave a soft cry of protest as he lifted her up in his arms; he ignored it and carrying her across to the chaise-longue beneath the window set her down on it and sat beside her, leaning over her so that she was forced to lie still.

'Have you changed your mind?' he demanded in a low tone.

Isabel shook her head. Her fingers lightly touched the square-cut jaw above her and were immediately caught in a fierce grasp.

'Have you?' she asked quietly. 'Are you sure you really want me, James, and you aren't just being chivalrous because we were forced to spend a night alone together?'

'I could show you how much I want you, but that would put me in the same category as other men you have known, and I won't be like them.'

Isabel's face clouded at his reference to her past.

'I must tell you——' she began, but he silenced her with a shake of his head.

'No.'

'Then you will always wonder, won't you? How many men shared my bed or how many I gave myself to. No matter how hard you try you will always think of it and sometimes mention it with the same bitterness in your voice as just now.'

'I didn't mean to—I won't again. I have you now and I'll never let you go—that's all that matters. Now, give me your hand and let us go and tell Alistair our good news.'

'Poor Father. He will never live to see his grandson—perhaps not even our marriage,' Isabel said with trembling lips. 'Oh, James, if only he could see us wed.'

'I could have the minister here within three days if

you really wish it.' James held her close, aware she was
fighting to control a rush of tears, 'but I don't want it to
be like the last time. The villagers will make you the
most beautiful wedding dress ever seen. I'll fill this
house with so many guests, the celebrations will last for
a month, and I want to make De'n Ceo ready to receive
you.'

'It is—your mother saw to that. I want to spend my
wedding night in her apartments, James—do you
understand why? I would love to have it all the way you
say—but——'

'Do you think your father would mind? Let's go to
him and tell him of our plans—that alone will make
him happy, and then let providence take care of the
rest.'

Hand in hand they walked down the long corridor to
Alistair's room. He lay in the same lethargic state as
when Isabel had stayed with him earlier that day.

'Father.' Gently she took one of his hands and lightly
pressed it. To her surprise her father's eyes flickered
slowly open, and there was an answering pressure on
her fingers. James leant over the bed, his arm resting
around her shoulders. How comforting his touch was.
'Father—James and I have been making plans for our
wedding. Are you pleased? Say you are—it's what you
want, isn't it?'

A faint nod came from the weakened man before
them. Slowly, painfully, Alistair lifted Isabel's hand,
holding it out towards James, who took it and held it in
a firm grip.

'You should have married her six years ago, James.
Make up for those years of unhappiness—never hurt
her.'

The tired eyes closed again and for a moment Isabel
felt panic, but James smiled, reassuring her that he was
only asleep, and led her out of the room.

For over an hour they walked in the garden. Autumn

was fast approaching and the last of the flowers Isabel
loved so much were disappearing. She stopped to pluck
a last rose and enjoy its sweet fragrance.

'At your wedding you shall have a bouquet of the
most beautiful roses I can find,' James said with a
smile.

'No—just one—a red rose.'

'Anything to make you happy. Despite everything we
will be happy, Isabel, I swear it.'

"Despite everything"—even those innocent words
had an ominous ring to them, she thought.

'If your father was not ill,' James went on, 'there
would be a long-drawn-out engagement—under the
circumstances I think we should set the wedding day
for a month hence. Do you agree?'

Her lips were soft and clinging as James drew her
beneath the shelter of some trees and kissed her.

'Shall I make the arrangements with the
minister—for the last Friday in September?'

'Yes, James—oh, yes.' She kissed him again and
clung to him almost desperately. 'Come and see me
again soon—I missed you yesterday.'

Slight though it was, she felt James stiffen and looked
up enquiringly into his face. He was no longer smiling
and she drew back, asking quietly:

'What is it? What have I said?'

James looked down at her hands clasped tightly in
his. He pressed them tighter as if afraid she might run
from him when he gave an answer.

'I'll come again when I can. It may be a few days—it
depends.'

'On what? We have so much to talk about. I'm so
excited, James, like a little girl almost. Nothing on this
earth must spoil things for us.'

'Only Duncan can do that. I was out after him yesterday if you want the truth.'

The colour fled from Isabel's cheeks. Slowly she

withdrew her hands and stepped back, fighting down a sudden urge of panic.

'Why can't you leave him alone? Hasn't he suffered enough?'

'He killed my ward, Isabel. Brother or not—I have to avenge her. It's something you must accept.'

'I'll never accept it—or you if you harm him,' Isabel replied slowly.

James's hands clamped down so hard on her shoulders she winced.

'In a month's time you will be my wife and you'll damned well do as I say. Grow up, Isabel—you're no longer a child—neither is Duncan. He's a hunted murderer and I intend to catch him. Threaten me with anything you wish, but never try to carry it out. I'm not Julian de Riché—I'm a man, and in a month's time you'll find that out. Now I'll take my leave of you and first thing in the morning I'll ride over to see the minister.'

Without waiting for an answer he released her and strode off down the path, not even looking back when she called his name. She began to run after him, then stopped, her hands clenching into tight fists at her side. James was stubborn and so was she. He was soon to be her husband and Duncan was her brother. Was the bond of love stronger than that of blood?

CHAPTER
SEVEN

'APART from the few hours she spent with her father this morning, she's been in there—pining her heart out,' Simone muttered fiercely, jerking her head towards the closed door of Isabel's bedroom. She stared into Jean-Paul's emotionless face with angry eyes. 'The wedding date has been set, you know. In one month she may very well marry the man who will kill her brother.'

'Not any more. You know me well enough not to underrate my powers of persuasion, Simone. Less than ten minutes ago our friend downstairs was singing like a bird. Fetch Madame, she will want to hear what he has to say.'

'Madame! You haven't called her that for weeks.'

'I must remember my place now, mustn't I?' A tight smile tugged at the corners of Jean-Paul's mouth, but his sister noticed there was no humour in his dark eyes. '*Mon Dieu*, I hold her happiness in the palm of my hand, do you realise that? I have only to say that the man Beaton died without speaking and she would never dare marry the MacLeod for fear he discovered why she really returned from France. In time I would be able to persuade her to go home.'

'Where you would be available to console her.' Simone's lips deepened contemptuously. 'Love has addled your brains, my brother.'

'I've never loved a woman as I love her,' Jean-Paul returned in a fierce whisper, and his sister's momentary anger vanished at the sincerity in his voice.

'And she will love no other man as she loves James MacLeod. If she leaves him and goes back to France she will never forget him and I doubt if you are man enough to make her for less than a week. If she turned to you it would be out of desperation—is that what you want? You would destroy her and she would grow to hate you. Whether you admit it or not, you and the MacLeod are alike. You are both men of violent temperament, swift to anger, but slow to forgive, both of you have a gentler side of your nature which few people ever see. If the worst happens and she is forced to go home, she will need that gentleness, *mon frère*—and your help. I will never forgive you if you betray her trust.'

Jean-Paul's smile broadened as he turned from the fire to face his sister.

'Why, Simone! I do believe you thought I was serious. Go and wake her up before I give the matter serious consideration.'

Simone's hand was raised to knock at Isabel's door, but before she could do so it opened and her mistress stood before her. She threw a worried glance over her shoulder at Jean-Paul, wondering if their conversation had been overheard.

Isabel raised a hand to tidy her dishevelled hair. She was very pale and looked tired.

'I fell asleep,' she confessed, stepping into the room. 'Have you news, Jean-Paul?'

'The best, Madame. If you would like to come and hear it from the man Beaton himself——' he broke off as Isabel's eyes became alive with sudden hope.

'He talked?'

'Everything.'

'Tell me—for God's sake.'

'Your brother Duncan has killed no one. Kirsty Fraser was murdered by Malcolm and his steward was a witness.' Jean-Paul held out his hand towards her. 'Come and hear it for yourself.'

Unable to believe all her prayers were about to be answered, Isabel followed Jean-Paul down to the underground caves where he held his prisoner. Every step she took brought her nearer to clearing Duncan's name—and to an unshadowed marriage to James.

The tide had just gone out and the sand was still wet and soft. Jean-Paul lifted her from the stairs and carried her down a long tunnel which led deep into the honeycomb of caves. Behind them Simone muttered fiercely under her breath as she stumbled in the flickering light of the single wall torch and almost fell.

Andrew Beaton, bound and gagged, lay against the rock face. Beyond him was a wide chasm with the cold waters of the Atlantic still frothing over its edge on to the sand. He wore nothing except a pair of trousers and he was wet and shivering violently.

As Jean-Paul gently set her down, Isabel stared at the dark waters apprehensively. She knew every foot of the caves, including the one in which they now stood. At low tide it held no water and there was a narrow ledge halfway down the narrow opening. She had no doubt Andrew Beaton had been left on that stretch of rock to watch the incoming tide slowly, relentlessly creeping up the walls towards him. She had been prepared for Jean-Paul to torture him—yet somehow she wished he had not used this method. She knew the terrors of being trapped by the tide and suddenly shivered.

'The end justifies the means,' Jean-Paul said quietly. Reaching down her jerked the cloth from Andrew Beaton's mouth and ordered, 'Tell my mistress what you told me.'

There was silence and Isabel's heart sank at the stubborn look which crept into the hard face looking up at her. Had he found new courage to defy them—knowing they dare not kill him and lose the only witness to Malcolm's crime?

'Speak, my friend—or the next time I'll hang you over the edge by your thumbs,' Jean-Paul snapped.

The steward's complexion became grey with fear.

'My lady—mercy—for pity's sake don't let this madman drown me.'

'Then tell me the truth about Kirsty Fraser.' Stifling her conscience, Isabel remained composed. She was too close to achieving her aim to become weak now.

'If I don't talk he'll kill me,' Andrew Beaton muttered, jerking his head towards the man at her side. 'If I do, Lord Malcolm will.'

'I won't kill you,' Jean-Paul said, moving forward, 'but if you give me cause to grow angry you'll beg me for death.'

'I'll tell you——' Desperate eyes turned on Isabel, pleading. 'My lady, will you give me safe passage away from here?'

'You are in no position to make any bargains,' came Isabel's cold answer. 'Tell me what I want to know and I'll decide whether or not you have earned the right to go on living.'

'You believe the Lord Malcolm responsible for the killing of the Fraser girl—it's true, he is—he did it.'

'Why?'

'Because she was in love with your younger brother Duncan. The marriage was arranged by your father and James MacLeod, but she never loved Lord Malcolm. She told James MacLeod and asked him to release her, but he refused and so she and your brother planned to elope.'

'Malcolm found out and killed her,' Isabel whispered.

'Yes—I overheard them making plans and we laid in wait for them. Your brother Duncan was wounded, and when Kirsty Fraser tried to stop my lord killing him, he turned on her and killed her in a jealous rage. By the time I had brought him to his senses the other one had made good his escape, and curious servants were coming out to investigate all the noise——'

'And you concocted the story that Duncan had killed Kirsty when she refused his advances,' Isabel murmured. 'Yes—you are speaking the truth—it tallies with what my brother has already told me. So, Jean-Paul,' she turned and looked at him with a heavy sigh, 'it is over. We have won.'

'Not yet. First we have to prove it in a court of law, and to do so we must keep this man alive to repeat what he has told us. I'll find him some warm clothes, but I suggest you leave him down here where he won't be found. It would help too if you could get someone else in the house on your side.'

'Not my father; he is too ill to be troubled at the moment, even with such good news, but perhaps we could enlist Mary's help.'

'Can you trust her?' Simone asked with a frown. 'She is his wife, after all.'

'We must tell her. Go and fetch her here, Simone, but don't tell her why.' Isabel watched Jean-Paul examine the stout ropes binding his prisoner, and a grateful smile touched her pale face. 'Thank you, Jean-Paul—I can never repay you for this service.'

'Your happiness is my reward, you know that.' He straightened and came across to her. 'When I have seen this man is a little more comfortable and has eaten, I'll ride for your brother.'

'He is at the house in Inverness——'

'Then I will send one of his men to fetch him, I don't want to be away from you for too long—not until I'm sure Malcolm cannot harm you. On the way back, shall I tell James MacLeod our news and bring him here? He has sworn to kill the man who murdered his ward, and I think it only fair we should bring them face to face.'

'Will he believe me, Jean-Paul?'

'You above all people. He loves you, doesn't he?'

'Then bring him, but hurry——' She broke off with a shiver of apprehension which brought a troubled frown to the Frenchman's face. So she, too, was feeling uneasy. But why, when so much had been achieved? Impulsively he took her by the shoulders, smiling down into her troubled face.

'Courage, *ma petite*. One more day will see an end to this nightmare.'

'Bless you, Jean-Paul—you have done so much for me.'

'Rubbish! Coming back to this house was your idea. If you remember, I thought it a stupid and dangerous venture.'

'Yes, I recollect your words.' His objections had been voiced in far stronger language and it had been the first time he had ever deliberately opposed her, Isabel recalled. He had loved her even then—— Now each new move they made which brought them nearer to vindicating Duncan also took her further away from Jean-Paul. In a voice that was little more than a whisper she said, 'How could I have been so blind!'

'I am very adept at concealing my feelings when I want to,' Jean-Paul murmured. Gently his fingers smoothed back a stray lock of her hair, then slid down over the side of her face as if to imprint the memory of it in his mind, and the impersonal caress brought the sparkle of bright tears to her eyes. With an oath he gathered her against his chest, burying his face against the softness of her hair.

'Don't cry for me, I'm not worth it. Be happy with your James—as happy as I have been to serve you—protect you—love you.' Jean-Paul contained the flow of passionate words which leapt to his lips—he had no right to speak them to her now that her heart belonged to another man. For a long moment he held her in silence—knowing it might well be the last time they could be so openly honest with each other; grateful for the way she stayed quietly within the circle of his arms.

A soft footstep caused him to raise his head, and over

Isabel's shoulder he encountered the astounded gaze of Mary MacLeod and behind her his sister, her face clouded with suspicion by the sight which confronted her. He could have murdered them both for intruding on his very private moment.

'You want to see me,' Mary said, and her voice was cold.

'I need your help,' Isabel answered, perfectly composed. She stayed close beside Jean-Paul, unconcerned what might have been read into the scene the other woman had come upon. She nodded towards the bound figure on the ground a few feet away and watched Mary's face go white with fear as she recognised who it was.

'Are you mad? Why is Malcolm's steward being treated in such a fashion? If he finds him here——'

'Which he will not unless you tell him,' Isabel interrupted, 'and when you have heard what he has to say I doubt if you will ever want to see him again, let alone run to him with tales of my misdeeds. But first I think there is something you must know.'

'Is it wise to tell her everything?' Jean-Paul muttered, speaking in French so that Mary could not understand him.

'We can lose nothing by being honest with her,' Isabel answered. She turned back to Mary, her eyes searching the other's face as she spoke. 'Six months before I returned home, Duncan came to me in France to enlist my help in proving that he was innocent of Kirsty Fraser's murder. The story he told me is vastly different from Malcolm's.'

'Of course it is. It's a pack of lies.'

'Duncan's story has been corroborated—by him,' Isabel answered triumphantly, pointing towards Andrew Beaton. 'He was a witness to the whole thing. He saw Malcolm kill Kirsty in a jealous fit.'

'You lie!' Mary swayed backwards against the cave

wall, her senses reeling under Isabel's words. 'Malcolm
could never kill her—he loved her.'

'Perhaps—but I've never known him to love anyone.
Listen to his steward—I beg you.'

'To a confession extracted under torture?' Mary
demanded. 'Look at the man, he's half dead. He'll say
anything you want to stay alive.'

'Do you really think he would lie against your husband, my lady?' Jean-Paul interposed. 'He knows we
cannot kill him and lose the only witness to the
truth—he had only to keep silent——'

The commonsense of his words seemed to make an
impression on Mary. She crossed to where Andrew
Beaton lay and stared down at him apprehensively.

'Speak!' Jean-Paul stirred him none too gently with
his foot. Isabel cast a relieved look at Simone as the
steward began to relate, in the fullest detail, what had
happened on the night of the murder. She watched the
expression of disbelief on Mary's face change to one of
suspicion and then horror as doubts began to creep into
her mind.

'What if I believe this man?' she asked, without
looking around. She was very pale and the hands
clasped in front of her toyed nervously with the ends of
her scarf, but there was no sign of tears, which did not
unduly worry Isabel, who had expected none. Mary did
not love Malcolm, and Isabel doubted if her three short
months of marriage had been either successful or
happy, and although she probably had not seen the
worst of her husband's temper, she had seen sufficient
to know he was capable of great violence.

'I'm not asking you to testify against Malcolm—only
to help us keep Andrew Beaton alive to repeat what he
has told you to the sheriff in Inverness. Malcolm has
only to have the slightest suspicion of what we are about
and he'll kill me—and Jean-Paul and my maid—anyone who could betray him.'

'Would he kill me?' Mary swung around and stared at Isabel challengingly. 'Are you telling me I don't know my own husband? He has a temper, I admit, but he has always controlled it.'

'Always? Have you never argued? Has he never flown into a rage for no reason at all?'

'No—no—yes, we have argued, over you and Duncan mainly, and the way you shut him out as a child. I can't blame him for being bitter.'

'So you feel sorry for him, do you? Well, your sympathy is misplaced,' Isabel retorted. 'I don't suppose he's told you about the time he imprisoned me down here because I had upset him. Duncan found me in waist-deep water.'

'He—he didn't intend to let you drown, he would have come back.'

'After trapping me here he left the house to visit a girl in the village. He was still there when Duncan found me. I was left to drown, Mary—in cold blood. Perhaps with Kirsty it was different—perhaps he did have some feelings for her. In which case he would never have allowed her to look at another man, let alone break her engagement to marry Duncan. He has always hated Duncan because he is my favourite—as he was Father's long ago.'

'As he still is,' Mary intervened. 'Your father has forbidden his name in this house, but he has not stopped loving him. When he looks at Malcolm sometimes I'm sure he sees Duncan's face, and Malcolm knows how he feels—he's spoken of it often enough.'

'How does he speak of it?' Isabel prompted.

'With hatred in his eyes every time he mentions Duncan's name—and when he looks at you——' Mary broke off, pressing a hand to her temple. 'I don't know what to think. I want to believe you.'

'Trust me, that's all I ask—and let the sheriff and a jury decide whether Andrew Beaton's story is the truth

or not. I'm willing to stand by their decision—I only
want to give Duncan the chance to tell his side of it
without the risk of Malcolm's sword at his back,' Isabel
answered.

She stood with wildly beating heart as Mary's eyes
slowly searched her face, then moved to Jean-Paul's
stony features and the hand which rested on the hilt of
the knife in his belt. She turned to contemplate the
silent figure at her feet before asking:

'What do you want me to do?'

'I have to ride to De'n Ceo to bring back James
MacLeod before we move Beaton to a safer
place—with his help we will be sure of getting him out
alive. My sister will bring food down here—you will
keep watch and ensure no other servants are about.'

Jean-Paul spoke before Isabel could give an answer.
She thought he was being over-cautious by not men-
tioning he was also sending word to Duncan. He obviously did not fully trust Mary, but she did. She felt sorry
for her and the predicament she was now in. Impulsively she went to her and putting her arms around her
kissed her on the cheek.

'I'm sorry to hurt you this way——'

'You must do what you see fit to protect those you
love,' Mary answered in an odd tone. 'I shall be in my
rooms if you need me again. If you send your maid,
Malcolm will not become suspicious; he's used to
seeing her attend me.'

'Thank you, Mary,' Isabel said gratefully. Taking
down the wall-torch, Simone led the way out of the cave
and Mary followed without a backward glance.

'I don't trust her,' Jean-Paul muttered.

'What would you suggest we do—tie her up down
here too?' Isabel asked, slightly annoyed by his attitude.

'Your life is in danger if she talks.'

'It always has been—since the first moment I stepped into the house again. Malcolm has never really

believed I came home because I was bored with Versailles, and he's had Beaton watching me.'

'So when he's missed he'll turn on you?'

'Perhaps—he'll watch me for sure, but I shall remain in my rooms or with Father and he will find nothing unusual in my actions. Simone and Mary will be able to come and go as they please until you return. Go now, Jean-Paul, and ride swiftly.'

Jean-Paul bent low over her hand for a long moment and she did not see the look of apprehension which masked his dark features. He was used to death and had seen it many times during his turbulent childhood, and he had killed several men during his thirty-odd years, two of them since he joined Isabel's service—but never before had he felt so close to death himself. With an effort he contained the icy shiver running along his spine—it was like being touched by the hand of Death herself.

It was midnight as Mary opened the door of her room and stepped out into the shadowy corridor. For over three hours she had been sitting in a chair beside the window, waiting patiently for the servants to go to bed and praying Malcolm might put in an unexpected appearance, but he had not come. She had seen Jean-Paul ride away from the house just as it was growing dark and heaved a silent sigh of relief. He frightened her—the way he had looked at her in the underground cavern told her he would have killed—or at least imprisoned her if she had not agreed to help Isabel.

Andrew Beaton had spoken the truth. She had always suspected that he and Malcolm had conspired together to hide the true facts of Kirsty Fraser's death, but it was no longer important. Malcolm had loved Kirsty and Kirsty had loved Duncan, the quiet, studious Duncan with his perfect manners, the favourite at Asher Mor.

And Mary? Mary had loved Malcolm from the first moment she was introduced to him at the home of James MacLeod. She had watched him dancing with Kirsty and felt as if her heart would break. She had seen the usually placid Duncan give way to anger without realising, at that moment, the cause. How neatly everything fitted into place now! And now Mary was to have a child—a son perhaps, which would bind her to Malcolm—in time he might even grow to love her, too.

Quietly Mary stole along to her husband's apartments, pausing for a moment before opening the door and slipping inside without knocking. For the sake of her unborn child she had come to a desperate decision.

Isabel yawned and stretched her cramped arms. She had fallen asleep in a chair beside her father's bed and awakened to find the cold grey light of morning creeping through the unshuttered windows. Alistair MacLeod still slept. He had not known her when she relieved a weary Lachlan and sat beside him, nor spoken during the long hours before her eyes closed from sheer exhaustion. Sometimes she felt sure he would drift away in one of his deep sleeps without ever speaking again—without knowing how she had succeeded in vindicating Duncan.

Creeping to the door, she quietly eased it open and closed it with the same caution behind her. There was time to snatch a few hours' sleep in her own bed before Jean-Paul returned with James. Two shadowy figures can out of a side room as she neared her apartments. Even as she realised they had been in Simone's room and turned to question them, a rough hand closed over her mouth and someone grabbed both her arms, pinioning them behind her back so that she was helpless. Half dragged, half carried, she was borne along the corridor and into her own sitting-room where she was thrown headlong to the floor.

A familiar sardonic laugh rang in her ears as she sat up, rubbing her bruised wrists, and she grew cold with fear at the sight of Malcolm perched on the arm of the couch a few feet away. Instinct told her everything had gone wrong, yet she could not determine how. She glanced back towards the door in time to see the two servants who had manhandled her go out, closing and locking the door behind them. Beyond Malcolm was her bedroom and the tiny gun hidden beneath her pillow, but the door to that room was closed too, and one look at the riding-whip in her brother's hand told her she would never reach it.

Isabel knew what he meant to do by the way he moved purposefully towards her, but there was no escape from the savage blows rained on her body. She threw up her hands to protect her face, falling to the floor in a huddle in an attempt to escape his brutality.

It was impossible for her to tell how many times she lost consciousness or dragged herself back through the maze of pain to more blows—more pain, but there came a time when she opened her eyes and found she was alone. She lay where Malcolm had left her, too dazed and weak to even lift her head.

'Thank God you are alive, I thought he'd killed you.' Simone brushed away the huge tears rolling down her cheeks and concentrated on the task of bathing her mistress's face.

Isabel's head was cradled in Simone's lap. She still lay in the sitting-room where her maid had found her almost an hour before.

'Jean-Paul,' Isabel whispered, 'you must warn him. If he tries to reach Beaton, Malcolm will know. He will set men to watch him.'

'If only I could, but we are locked in, and there are guards outside the door.'

Isabel struggled painfully to sit up as memory

crowded back, but the effort was too great and she fell back with a sob, moaning:

'James mustn't come here. Malcolm will twist everything I say to suit his own ends. Oh, God, after all we have done! We have lost, Simone, and Malcolm has won, as always. He will destroy us——'

'Hush, *mignonne*, don't distress yourself,' Simone begged. Carefully she raised Isabel into a sitting position, her mouth tightening into a grim line at the blood-red weals across her shoulders and arms. There were large bruises on her cheeks where she had been slapped and a graze on one temple where she had fallen against a chair. 'Gently—let me lift you. There now—don't worry, I have hold of you.'

Luckily Simone was a strong woman, for Isabel was unable to stand or walk by herself. Half an hour later she was tucked up in bed, her outraged body bathed and anointed with healing ointment, which momentarily helped to ease the pain. Wordlessly she had swallowed the glass of brandy Simone held to her lips and then collapsed half-insensible on to the pillows. Turning away from the bed, Simone went to stand by the window and watch the activity in the courtyard. Men had been riding in and out since it had been light, but they came and went in a strange silence. She had discovered the reason from the guard who had released her from her room to attend Isabel, and the news had brought about a sense of foreboding—the same uneasy feeling that Jean-Paul had mentioned before leaving her.

As Isabel tossed sleeplessly a few feet away, Simone began to pray to God to somehow deliver them all from the black-hearted monster who now ruled Asher Mor without anyone to question his authority—for less than two hours after Isabel had left him, Alistair MacLeod had died peacefully in his sleep.

CHAPTER
EIGHT

DISMOUNTING from his horse, James strode through the main doors and stood looking around the Great Hall in puzzlement. Asher Mor was as quiet as a graveyard and he shivered inexplicably. He swung round on Jean-Paul who entered behind him with Bran Mac-Kay, ordering:

'Find your mistress and tell her I am here. If she is so anxious to see me I should have expected her to be waiting.'

'Madame has had a very exhausting time since you last saw her,' the Frenchman retorted, stepping past him. His hand fell to the sword at his side as he moved forward. He, too, had expected Isabel to be waiting, and was again plagued with uneasiness. He had taken less than a dozen cautious steps up the staircase when two shadowy figures came down to meet him. He heard a muttered oath behind him and turned, drawing his weapon, to confront Malcolm and several more men, but a savage blow on the back of the head sent him crashing unconscious to the floor before he had a chance to use it.

'Lock him up and guard him well. I shall need to question him later,' Malcolm ordered. He was smiling as he turned to his visitor. 'James—Isabel told me she had sent for you. Come and have a drink, you look tired.'

He turned away and went into the drawing-room, not waiting for an answer. James watched Jean-Paul being unceremoniously dragged away before turning on his heel and, following, demanded irritably:

'What the devil's going on here?'

'It's a personal matter—you will know everything in time,' Malcolm answered, holding out a glass of whisky to him. 'Take it, James, you'll have need of much more before the day is over.'

'Where's Isabel?—I want to see her.'

'She is in her room—a trifle indisposed.'

James's eyes narrowed sharply.

'What have you done to her?'

'I was afraid you were beginning to believe her wild tales. You've grown soft, my friend. I preferred the way you were with her when she first came back—at least then you were a man and not her slave. She has enough of those—both men and women.'

James slammed down his glass so hard that whisky splashed on to the table. There was a noticeable flush beneath his dark cheeks.

'I didn't come here to listen to you slander my future wife. Send someone to fetch her, or I'll go to her room.'

'First I suggest you go and pay your respects to an old friend,' Malcolm returned calmly. 'My father died earlier this morning.'

'My God, you are a black-hearted swine,' James swore. 'I believe you are glad he's dead.'

'Of course. I've been waiting for this moment for years—waiting for the time when I shall rule Asher Mor and everyone beneath its roof. Guard your tongue, James—don't make an enemy of me, you have enough problems.'

James did not hear the last threatening words, he was already striding across the Great Hall and at the bottom of the stairs he encountered Lachlan.

'Is it true?'

'Aye, my lord. The master is dead.' The old man was very pale and unusually nervous. He looked around him, his expression guarded, then moved closer to James.

'Lady Isabel has need of you. Go to her.'

'In a while. First I must go to Alistair—he was a good friend.'

'You must befriend the living now, not the dead,' Lachlan whispered. 'Go to her, I beg of you, before it is too late.'

'Isabel is probably sleeping,' came Malcolm's voice from behind James. 'She is in no condition to be disturbed—by anyone. Why aren't you with your master, Lachlan? There are things to be done.'

'I have to go out.' Slowly Lachlan came across the Great Hall to where Malcolm stood. 'I need fresh heather. The master always wore a sprig of heather in his bonnet ever since he was a lad. I want him to look right at the last.'

'Nonsense—get back where you belong.'

'Let the old man go, he has that right. He served Alistair long before you were born,' James interrupted angrily. 'Go, Lachlan—find your heather.'

'Thank you, my lord.' The man hurried away before any more could be said on the subject. James glared at Malcolm, daring him to pursue the argument, his temper roused by such a show of pettiness, but there was no further comment and he continued upstairs with a heavy heart.

It was beginning to rain as Lachlan crossed the drawbridge and walked as quickly as his tired old legs could manage towards the moors, but once out of sight of Asher Mor he drew his plaid more firmly about him and turned purposefully in the direction of the village.

When James returned to the sitting-room he found it deserted. A tray of fresh drinks had been left on the table and he lost no time in opening a new bottle of whisky.

By the time Malcolm joined him he had consumed

two-thirds of the bottle beside him. The mixture of liquor and the shock of the death of a close friend had plunged him into a black mood, exactly as Malcolm had foreseen. He had planned a careful sequence of events, first making sure James would be vulnerable to his unscrupulous scheme.

Pouring himself some brandy he stood before James's chair and stared at the silent figure for a long while, contemplating his next move. James glanced up as his empty glass was refilled, unaware before that moment of Malcolm's presence. His eyes instantly grew dark with anger and he stood up, putting the drink to one side without touching it.

'I will see Isabel and then I will leave,' he said curtly.

'As you wish. You will be attending the funeral?'

'Of course, but after Isabel and I are married I will have no reason to come here again. You and I have nothing in common.'

'Except a vow of vengeance. Have you forgotten your oath sworn over Kirsty's grave? Duncan still lives and instead of hunting him you allow yourself to be swayed from your pledge by my innocent-faced whore of a sister, whose sole reason for returning to Asher Mor was to prove me a liar. You were not the only one taken in—she fooled Father, too. Thank God he's dead—now I can deal with her my way and without interference——'

He broke off at the rising anger on James's face, and was not quick enough to evade the hand which snaked out and fastened on to the front of his coat. He was borne backwards on to the couch and pinned down by James's knee against his chest.

'If I thought you'd dare harm her I'd slit your throat here and now,' James swore between clenched teeth.

'Save your anger for Duncan and her. She's tricked you—led you on to believe she loves you so that she can persuade you to stop hunting her beloved brother.'

Malcolm's face was rapidly growing redder at the fierce, unrelenting pressure on his chest. At his words James's hands moved to grip his throat and further interfere with his breathing in a very effective way. Malcolm closed pain-racked eyes against the murderous face hovering over him. He had misjudged the depths of James's love. If he could not turn it to his advantage, his life was forfeit.

'She has my steward—imprisoned somewhere in the house. She took Mary into her confidence——' his voice trailed off as the agonising grip on his wind-pipe increased—then abruptly it ceased and he lay dazed and gasping for breath. Roughly James hauled him upright, demanding:

'Mary! Have you involved her in your schemes now?'

'She will tell you as I do—that Isabel and her French lover have imprisoned Beaton—tortured him to make him tell a pack of lies.'

'Lies—or the truth.' James stepped back, his eyes blazing with a mixture of anger and disbelief. His first reaction was the latter. Isabel loved him—he had held her in his arms and she had been warm and alive, welcoming his kisses—wanting to give him not only her lips but her body. He had felt it, but because he loved her too he had denied himself that pleasure.

He did not see the smile which touched Malcolm's face as he picked up the drink he had earlier refused and tossed it back in one swallow. The liquor he had consumed was having the desired effect after all—it had inflamed his senses sufficiently to arouse his suspicions. Mary's testimony would brand Isabel as a liar, if not more, and Andrew Beaton would turn the tide completely against her, Malcolm thought with malicious satisfaction.

'Will you hear me out?' He stood up, careful to stand well out of reach.

'Say what you have to and then bring Isabel here to answer your accusations, if you dare!'

'That is my intention, James! Listen to me—you were right about her from the start. She lied and cheated her way through the court at Versailles for years—God knows how many lovers she's had. You must not blame yourself for being duped—others have gone before you. I was one—I really believed she had come back because she loved her home and Father. God help him, looked on her as the same innocent child who went away. She's an evil, calculating witch—she came back with only one purpose in mind—to bribe or frighten witnesses to lie in favour of Duncan.

'He went to her in Paris last year, you know. When she stepped off the boat in Scourie she was in possession of all the facts and from the beginning she lied. Didn't she, James? Didn't she lie to you—pretending there were other reasons for her return?'

'Let her tell me herself.' James was very pale and the fingers purposefully clutching the hilt of his sword tightened until the knuckles grew white. It was the only outward sign of his torment, but it was enough for Malcolm to recognise the seeds of suspicion were now firmly sown.

'If that is the only way to convince you, so be it. I'll have her brought down.'

'If it was his horse you saw he must have been waylaid by Lord Malcolm,' Simone declared, moving back from the window.

'It was James,' Isabel said adamantly. She was seated before the dressing table, fully dressed after only a few hours' sleep. 'Come and do my hair. Does my face look all right?' Simone inspected the heavy powder which successfully hid the bruises on her mistress's cheeks and her mouth deepened in distaste. Isabel held out a pair of brushes with a faint smile. 'Don't say it—I know I look like some of the women at court, but I don't want James to know what has happened. He would kill Malcolm.'

'He will sooner or later—why not get it over with now and be done with it?'

'I want Malcolm to come to trial and publicly clear Duncan. I don't want blood on my hands or on James's. There—now I look presentable.'

Isabel stood up and swayed unsteadily for a moment as pain seared through her body. Waving aside Simone's outstretched hands she limped into the drawing-room, but before she could sit down the sound of the door being opened made her look up, expecting to see James's tall frame in the doorway. Somehow she managed to hide her apprehension at the sight of the two clansmen confronting her.

'Lord Malcolm wants you downstairs,' one of them growled in a surly voice. 'Just you—the other woman stays here,' he added as Simone stepped forward.

'I will not——' the maid began, but Isabel warned her to silence. She had hoped to win some of the servants over to her side, but these men Malcolm had chosen to be her guards were obviously hand-picked and completely loyal. Her brother had thought of everything. Thank heaven Jean-Paul had brought James. She was halfway down the stairs before she found herself wondering why neither of them had come to see her.

'In here.' She was ushered into the library by her guards and left alone. She did not bother to open the door and check whether they were outside because she knew they were. From the far side of the room she heard a sharp intake of breath and as she spun around was caught up in Jean-Paul's arms.

'Isabel—*m'amie*—you are safe.' His mouth on hers stilled Isabel's answer and he was oblivious to her protests until she pressed her hands against his chest and tried to push him away. 'Forgive me, I've been out of my mind with worry. No sooner had I returned than I was seized and thrown into a filthy dungeon. No one would tell me what had happened to you——' he broke off, his fingers lightly touching her face. 'My poor little love, no amount of powder can hide the fact you've been crying for hours.'

'Don't talk to me like that, Jean-Paul—you mustn't.'

'Why not? Just because my love for you must be denied, that doesn't make it any the less important than that of James MacLeod.'

'James——' Isabel scarcely heard his words. She could only think of the way the man she loved was at Asher Mor, but had not attempted to see her. 'Have you seen him?'

'He came back with me, that's all I know. I expect he went to pay his last respects to your father. Did you manage to tell him of your success before the end?'

Isabel looked at him blankly, then as his words penetrated her troubled mind, she clutched at him, crying out:

'What are you saying? The end—no, Jean-Paul, not my father!'

'Dear God, has no one told you?' Fierce expletives fell from the Frenchman's lips as she sagged half fainting in his arms. Lifting her back on to the couch, he settled her head on a cushion and gently stroked the loose hair away from her face. So intent was he on his ministering that neither he or the grief-stricken Isabel heard the door carefully open or saw the three figures who stood on the threshold silently watching—listening. 'He died last night, *m'amie*—in his sleep.'

'But I was with him——' Isabel's voice trailed off into a miserable silence. Her father had died while she slept in the chair and she had left him without realising what had happened. 'I didn't tell him—I didn't want to disturb him. When I was returning to my room Malcolm's men grabbed me and took me to him.'

'He knows of Beaton?'

'He never mentioned him—he couldn't know.'

'Then why did he choose that time to show his hand —unless, of course, he knew your father was dead and he was in command.'

'Yes—yes, that must be it. Thank God we are still safe.' Isabel laid her head against Jean-Paul's shoulder, fighting to keep back her tears. 'How can I think of my own safety when my father lies dead upstairs? I am shameless.'

'No—*m'amie*—human. He lived a good full life—he would never have denied you the same right. Courage now, we still have Malcolm to face.'

'And James MacLeod,' came the biting answer from behind them. 'You are as good as dead, Frenchman.'

Jean-Paul leapt to one side, his hand falling to his side before realising he had no weapon. James stood behind the couch—on either side of him Malcolm and Mary. Too late he recognised the trap that he and Isabel had unsuspectingly triggered. The news of her father's death had been deliberately withheld from her and then they had been left alone together for him to break it to her—to comfort her as someone had known he would. His accusing eyes centred on Mary, who coloured and quickly looked away.

'You treacherous bitch,' Jean-Paul muttered. 'You have betrayed us.'

'No—no, you are mistaken, Mary is with us.' Isabel dragged herself from the couch and stretched out her hands towards James. 'Thank God you are here. Why didn't you come to me?'

'I was with your father. Malcolm led me to believe you were indisposed—I understand why now,' James answered. He did not look at her but at the man at her side, and his expression told her the thoughts in his mind.

'Perhaps you can tell me, then,' Isabel snapped back, both alarmed and hurt by his rejection. 'I asked Jean-Paul to bring you to me so that I could prove to you once and for all Duncan is innocent of the murder of Kirsty Fraser. What did you think you witnessed, James?'

'I saw a tearful woman being comforted by her servant lover,' Malcolm broke in. 'Why bother to deny it any longer, Isabel? I can bring servants who have seen him coming out of your room in the early hours of the morning.'

'And all of them afraid of you,' Isabel challenged.

'Are you placing me in that category?' Mary asked. She was standing very close to Malcolm and when she hesitated he turned and looked at her and half smiled as if to reassure her. 'I believed you at first, too—I could not believe you guilty of the life Malcolm spoke of—but watching you with—with that man—seeing him leaving your room! Can you deny that I saw you in his arms only yesterday?'

'Can you?' James demanded when Isabel did not answer. He wanted to grab hold of her and shake her until she confessed it was the truth—at the same time praying for her to melt into his arms and persuade him it was a lie. Slowly she lifted her eyes to meet his.

'I am not on trial. What my brother and his wife believe is their affair—I will explain nothing to you now, James. If you love me, trust me—or has your great love fallen at the first hurdle? You once told me the past was forgotten. Words, James, mere words!'

'Very well, Isabel—I will hear you out, but first answer me one question. Did Duncan visit you in Paris and tell you of Kirsty's death?'

Momentary alarm leapt to Isabel's eyes. Apart from

her close servants and Mary, no one knew of the incident—except for Andrew Beaton, who had been lying only a few feet from them when she had mentioned it the previous day. Mary and Andrew Beaton! She raised questioning eyes to the silent figure of her sister-in-law and once again Mary avoided looking at her.

'Who told you? Mary?'

'No, Malcolm. Is it true?'

'Yes. I came back to Asher Mor to prove Duncan's innocence.'

'By any means in your power,' James added heavily, 'and that apparently meant deceiving not only your father but me. Was I easier than the others?'

'I admit I lied, but only about my reasons for returning,' Isabel answered, bright colour flooding her cheeks. She felt suddenly drained of all strength and her body ached from Malcolm's beating, yet somehow she retained her poise. Pride forbade her to throw herself into James's arms and beg him to believe her—the same pride which kept him from stretching out his hands and telling her that the past was forgotten. Her heart sank at the cold expression which settled over his face. 'You don't believe me, do you?'

'Do you care? Surely Duncan is the only one who has ever mattered to you?'

'James—James—can't you see what is happening to us? Look at Malcolm's face—he is enjoying this. We are doing what he wants, destroying everything good we had because of the suspicions he has planted in your mind.'

'You began the process with your first lie.'

Isabel started towards him, but at the first step Jean-Paul caught her wrist and pulled her back beside him, his black eyes glittering angrily.

'*Mon Dieu*, I've heard enough. Are you blind, Highlander? She'd crawl to you on her knees if she thought you'd believe her, but I won't let that happen—men like you have abused her enough in the past. Let him think what he pleases,' he turned on Isabel as she began to protest. 'You came back to prove Duncan's innocence and you have—tell him and let him go. He isn't worthy to kiss the hem of your gown.'

Isabel nodded, unaware of the agony in James's eyes. By her refusal to reprimand the Frenchman, as she would any servant who spoke to her in such a fashion, she was condemned. James was a man who had never known jealousy, but in that moment it surged through him like an uncontrollable fire, and only with a supreme effort did he quell the impulse to kill both Isabel and her lover.

'Andrew Beaton is imprisoned in the old smugglers' caves,' Isabel said at length. 'He will tell you all you want to know, James. Go to him—hear the truth of what happened that night.'

'Perhaps I can save you a wasted journey,' Malcolm drawled. Stepping in front of James who had turned towards the door, he flung it open and motioned to the three silent men standing in the Great Hall. A stifled scream broke from Isabel's lips at the sight of the man lying on the floor at their feet. It was Andrew Beaton—and his throat had been cut.

Mary stifled a gasp of horror behind her hands. She had known where Malcolm had gone the night before, but she had not been prepared for this.

'You killed him—to stop him talking.' Isabel wheeled on Malcolm, suddenly cold with fear, and her accusing eyes fell on Mary. 'She told you.'

'Supposing someone gives me an explanation,' James demanded. 'Is this your witness, Isabel?'

'Yes,' her answer was so low he could hardly hear it. 'Malcolm has had him murdered.'

'No—it was not Malcolm!' Mary stepped forward, nervously twisting her hands in front of her. 'You mustn't listen to her, James. She had me go down to the caves to hear Beaton's confession. He had been tortured, but when he saw me he swore he had told nothing but the truth before. Despite everything they had done to him he still maintained Duncan had killed Kirsty——'

'You lying bitch——' Jean-Paul's self-control broke. He started forward but was suddenly menaced by the point of James's sword against his chest. He stopped abruptly, cursing because he had no weapon.

'I need no excuse to kill you. If you think she is worth it we will fight later, but now I want to hear the truth of this affair,' James said in a fierce whisper. 'Go on, Mary.'

'When Beaton refused to change his story Isabel flew into a rage and ordered the Frenchman to kill him. She was beside herself. I don't really think she knew what she was doing.' Mary held her ground as James's merciless gaze searched her face, adding, 'You know how it is between Malcolm and myself, James—the marriage was not of our choice. I have no reason to lie and send an innocent man to his death.'

'No—no, you haven't,' James muttered. With something resembling a groan he turned away and began cursing vehemently under his breath. He heard a cry of alarm and swiftly spun round, his sword raised, suspecting treachery. His face white with rage, Jean-Paul had pushed Isabel to one side as she tried to stop him and leapt at Mary, his fingers closing around her throat. The swift flow of French which fell from his lips was lost on James, who stood momentarily too stunned to realise what was happening. Men dashed in from the Great Hall to drag him away, but Malcolm moved more quickly. As Mary sagged half fainting, he sank his dirk deep into Jean-Paul's back again and again until the man released his hold and fell to the floor where he lay in a pool of his own blood.

'Damn you, he wasn't armed,' James began, then

broke off as Isabel flung herself on her brother, screaming at him hysterically and raking at his cheeks with her
nails. Malcolm caught her by the arm and sent her
reeling back into the arms of the waiting clansmen and
then turned his attention to Mary, who was holding
both hands to her bruised throat and sobbing quietly.

'Do you see now what kind of woman she is?' he
demanded of James.

With a moan Isabel sagged in the grasp of the men
who held her, brought to a point of absolute despair by
James's silence. He looked at her as if he hated her.
Malcolm's twisted smile swam before her tortured
vision.

'Murderer,' she screamed at him. 'Haven't you done
enough to me without this?'

She closed her eyes, fighting to conquer the terrible
sickness which rose in her stomach as she stared down
into Jean-Paul's lifeless face. She opened them on to
James's face, dark with accusation.

'Why are you so upset over the death of this man? He
was only a servant,' he taunted.

What did he want her to say? Isabel wondered. With
Malcolm's help he had already made up his mind.

'Jean-Paul was much more than that, he was my
friend,' she returned, determined not to betray the trust
of the gallant man who had died in her defence. He had
shared her trust for so many years, asking nothing in
return except to serve her. Yet James, who professed to
love her dearly, had already condemned her on the
evidence of a pack of lies. In a low voice she added, 'You
wouldn't understand what I mean, James.'

'You see—she admits he was something to her. I told
you in the beginning that she was a whore, but you
wouldn't listen.'

James glared at him, fighting hard to control his
temper.

'What are you going to do with her?'

'Use her—to bait a trap for Duncan.'

James nodded, deliberately hardening his heart against the tear-stained face turned in his direction. If he looked into those tawny eyes he was lost, for they reminded him of so many tender moments. Tenderness—love—he was done with both.

'Do what you please with her, she means nothing to me,' he answered cruelly. 'If I lay hands on her again it will be to kill her.'

He heard Isabel cry out and the sound of a blow as he turned away, but he did not look back. He had done with pity, too.

The funeral of Alistair MacLeod took place two days later. Attired in his best plaid, his huge broadsword buckled around his waist and silver-crested sgian-dhu in his stocking, he was laid to rest on the hill behind Asher Mor, beside Suzanne his beloved wife and many of his ancestors. The day was dull and overcast and the villagers, who stood at a respectful distance around the grave, did so with heads downbent, suspecting an ill omen in the ever-darkening sky.

Accompanied by his steward, Bran MacKay, James arrived at Asher Mor as the funeral cortège was about to leave. He nodded briefly in the direction of Mary, but totally ignored Malcolm and the heavily veiled figure of Isabel, and rode directly behind the coffin. At the bottom of the hill the horses were tethered and everyone continued on foot. He noticed Isabel falter as she neared the graveside, only to be urged on callously by her brother, and brutally he squashed the impulse to go to her and give her his arm. Her grief was not real but a front to arouse sympathy from the watching villagers, most of whom, he knew, preferred Duncan to Malcolm, their new laird.

He had spent two long days shut up in his room at De'n Ceo, in a deliberate attempt to harden himself for this day. The sight of her tears as she raised the dark veil meant nothing to him—his love for her was dead. More than just his friend Alistair was being buried—with him went his hopes for a grandchild and James's shattered dreams for the future.

He had never made plans for the future before—never known how pleasant it was to dream of a wife and family—to fill his empty world which had been so desolate since the death of his parents. His various *affaires* had been short-lived and meaningless, and always De'n Ceo had been uppermost in his thoughts.

Isabel had changed all that—his life would never be the same, even now that he knew the truth about her. He had put her out of his life, but it would be a long time before he succeeded in putting her out of his mind.

Lachlan moved closer to Isabel as she leaned forward to toss a handful of earth on to the coffin. He had been following close behind her since leaving the house, but she had not noticed him.

'Come, my lady—let me help you back to the horses,' he murmured, taking her arm.

'No—no, I want to stay here,' Isabel answered, try-ing to pull free, but he held fast and as she turned on him, a sharp comment rising to her lips, she saw the slight inclination of his head. He wanted her to leave the graveside—to get away from the others—but for what reason? Simone took her other arm and, ignoring her faltering steps, drew her gently but firmly away. Malcolm motioned to the two clansmen nearest and they turned and followed the trio down the slope.

'I hate him,' she whispered under her breath. Her father was dead, she was her brother's prisoner, still stiff and aching from his beating and in fear of her life, and Duncan was still a fugitive—all because she had fallen in love.

'Who—your brother or James MacLeod?' Simone

asked. She was dressed from head to toe in black and heavily veiled. Beneath the covering her face bore little trace of the tearful hours she had spent since Jean-Paul had died. Already she was making plans to avenge him as she knew he would do if she had been killed so treacherously. She was a product of the gutters of Paris and that was the way she would fight—dirty.

'Both of them.'

'Love didn't come easily to ye and it will prove stronger than any hatred ye may think ye have for him now,' Lachlan muttered fiercely. 'It would be better if ye could hate him——'

Isabel's answer died on her lips. They had reached the tethered horses, watched over by two MacLeods and the familiar face beneath one of the bonnets brought a soft cry to her lips. As Lachlan helped her to mount her guards pushed Simone aside as if to pull her down again. Both of them died quickly and silently on the dirks of Duncan and his companion. As a shout of alarm came from the hill, Duncan flung himself on to his horse, urging the other before him and scattered the remaining horses which could be used to pursue them, before galloping after his sister.

The whole incident was executed so swiftly and neatly that no one even managed to fire a shot after the fleeing fugitives, and by the time the horses had been rounded up it was obvious it was too late to follow.

Malcolm raged and cursed until the clansmen thought he would throw a fit.

Watching him, Mary found a sickness rising in her stomach, not due to the child within her. The look on her husband's face was proof of the terrible wrong she had done to Isabel. No matter what kind of woman she was, she did not deserve to be hunted down like an animal and subjected to terrible indignities before she died, which was what Malcolm intended for her. And why? Was it only because she preferred Duncan, or was there a deeper, more recent, explanation—one she had refused to accept from the beginning? She had been the cause of the Frenchman's death with her lies—and destroyed James's love for Isabel and sent him on a path which was leading to more pain and death—all this because she had fallen in love with Malcolm and been determined to bring a grandson into the world for Alistair MacLeod.

Even that was unimportant now he was dead. Love had dragged Mary into a whirlpool of lies and deceit, trapping her because of her unborn child. The thought that it might inherit Malcolm's violent nature made her shudder with fear. From the bottom of the hill she could hear him shouting at his men, still swearing at them for their incompetence. Her face was wet with tears as she walked slowly down to join him.

CHAPTER
NINE

THE wall directly in Isabel's line of vision was green with moss and the previous night, when there had been a torrential storm, she had lain awake and watched the water dripping down on to the ground. Her clothes still felt damp from the headlong ride from the graveside to the safety of the cave which now sheltered them. She lay watching the men clustered around the small fire a few yards away. They all looked desperately tired yet, seeing she was awake, they smiled or nodded in her direction, and her heart warmed towards them. Despite the fact she knew they were being hunted at that very moment, she felt safe with such loyal men to guard her.

Slowly she sat up, rubbing her cold hands together. A shadow fell across her, and Duncan knelt at her side and caught her wrists with lean brown fingers. Clearly visible on her skin were some of the bruises Malcolm had inflicted.

'Simone told me you had been beaten,' he murmured, tight-lipped. 'Malcolm will answer to me with his life for this.'

'I saw you talking to her. What else did she say?'

'About her brother? Very little—can you talk about it? I must know what happened, Isabel. You don't know the torment I've been through since Lachlan sent word of Father's death and your imprisonment in the house. I sent men to watch and when they brought word that James had arrived I was sure he would take you to the safety of De'n Ceo—by force, if necessary.'

'James!' A bitter smile twisted Isabel's mouth as she

said the name, and Duncan sat back on his heels with a frown.

'So it's true—he has betrayed you?'

'Our love was never meant to be. I was stupid to believe him capable of trust, let alone love; he is only a man after all, and my experiences in France taught me that men will always lie and cheat to gain their own ends.'

'Tell me about—your experiences,' Duncan asked in a quiet voice.

Isabel looked at him in silence for a long while. Simone, who had been hovering nearby, making no attempt to hide the fact that she was listening to their conversation, came forward and bent over her mistress, putting her arms about her protectingly.

'Never ask her about the past,' she said fiercely.

'Stay out of this,' Duncan snapped, but he was glad that Isabel still had one staunch ally apart from himself.

'My brother has a right to know,' Isabel answered. 'Perhaps if I had told James the truth he would not have judged me so harshly.'

Her voice faltered and often broke and she revealed the secrets of her marriage to Julian and of the events which led up to her becoming a widow and the most popular topic of gossip, but he grew exceedingly pale and often cursed under his breath. Isabel spared herself nothing, although the revelations opened painful wounds and aroused memories best forgotten. She told him too how Jean-Paul had succeeded in making Andrew Beaton talk, only to be killed defending her when Malcolm once again twisted everything to his advantage.

'And how do you judge me?' she asked her brother with trembling lips.

'Judge you—my God, Isabel, what do you take me for? If I'd known what was happening Julian de Riché would have died by my hand before he could put any of his diabolical schemes into action. Why didn't you tell James?'

'Because at first I was too proud—and he made it quite clear when we met how he felt about me. Later, when he said he loved me, he said the past was forgotten. I meant to tell him everything after we were married. I was just happy because he loved me regardless of my scandalous life. My love made me oblivious to all the pitfalls. What a fool I was to think such happiness was for me.'

'He will know the truth before I kill him,' Duncan swore.

'No!' Isabel's eyes widened in sudden fear. 'I don't want your sympathy, Duncan—or only your understanding—and James's death will settle nothing. No matter how he feels towards me, I will always love him. I've tried to hate him, but it's beyond me.'

'If we are caught Malcolm won't spare either of us, and I have no reason to believe that James will be troubled by his conscience. I think it will be for the best if you return to France—I can arrange a passage.'

'No.'

'It will mean safety. I can follow as soon as Malcolm and I have settled our differences.'

'Oh, Duncan, I came back with such high hopes! I had the proof—how can I give up and go back to France? Even if you kill Malcolm you will still be a fugitive and blamed with two murders. You must stay and be master of Asher Mor—it was Father's wish before all this happened, you know that. The villagers need you, they have lived in fear long enough. I must stay, too.'

'To face James?'

'To be with you.' Isabel laid her aching head against Duncan's chest and was comforted by his arms holding her in a tight embrace. 'We will face Malcolm together. Win or lose, we will not be parted.'

'You are both mad,' Simone broke in, throwing up her hands in despair.

'No one is asking you to stay,' Duncan looked challengingly at the woman hovering over his sister. 'You are free to come and go as you please. You have served my sister well from what I've heard, and so I release you from her service without prejudice.'

'You release me?' Simone answered mockingly, contemplating the man before her. Not only was he good-looking but sure of himself, too, and she liked that. She had been aware of him watching her throughout the night as she kept a vigil over the sleeping Isabel, and for the first time in many years had been stirred by a man's interest. Since becoming Isabel's companion she had not been in love, and had been far too engrossed in looking after her young mistress to have any lovers. Now Duncan MacLeod had looked at her and she was remembering that she was a woman.

'Duncan is right, Simone, we have no right to place you in danger,' Isabel said.

'Have you forgotten that my brother is dead—murdered by your brother?' Simone demanded harshly. 'Do you think I will leave this land with him unavenged?'

'Malcolm belongs to me.' Duncan's eyes met hers challengingly.

'Only if you get to him first, monsieur,' came the infuriating reply before Simone moved away.

To Isabel's surprise, Duncan rose and followed her. At the entrance to the cave she stood aside to allow men to pass who had just returned from hunting and he stepped to her side, a restraining hand on her arm. She glanced down with a warning frown, but he held her fast.

'We are not in France now. You will not find assassins easy to hire. Yes, I know all about you—Isabel is very fond of you and I understand why now. She has a good friend in you. Perhaps you will be my friend, too, Simone? If we are to save Isabel further unhappiness we must not have different goals.'

'I want the man who killed my brother—dead.'

'He killed the woman I loved too, remember.'

'I was thinking about that when you stared at me last night,' Simone said, looking into the weatherbeaten face before her. 'You loved this Kirsty Fraser, yet you want me. Am I not correct?'

'Yes, I loved her and if she had not died we would be happily married now, living at Asher Mor—perhaps blessed with a child.' A shadow of pain crossed Duncan's face as he remembered the many plans he had shared with Kirsty. 'I'm a hunted man—wanted for a murder I did not commit. I've lived like an animal for nearly two years and my dreams have all turned to dust. I have no illusions about my future if I am caught, and that possibility at the moment is closer than ever before, despite anything I might say to Isabel. And so I live from day to day. Such an existence can be lonely——'

What was he asking of her? Simone wondered as he turned abruptly and went outside. An ally in the fight against his brother, or a companion to share his plaid at night? Whichever it was, the answer was the same.

For a week the cave was a safe refuge, but at last a chance encounter between Duncan's men cautiously out hunting and the MacLeods pursuing them forced the band to move on. From the mountains they came down to a friendly village, but after only a few hours' rest were surprised by a small group of James's men and a fierce fight followed, during which the horses were scattered and the survivors followed Duncan back into the hills, tired, hungry, many wounded—and on foot.

The intensity of the surprise attacks on their varied

hiding places continued until Isabel was afraid to close her eyes at night and the few hours' sleep she did have was plagued with nightmares. Everyone who sheltered them was put to the sword and their crofts burned—she had often crouched in the heather and watched the red flames searing the night sky. She forced herself to believe that it was Malcolm's work, not James's, although she knew both men had combined all their forces in the search for the fugitives. The luxury and comfort of France had made her forget how cruel her people could be, but lack of food and sleep was beginning to arouse memories of past clan wars when she was only a child—and of the Norsemen stories she had been told. James MacLeod was a descendant of such men, as proud and as ruthless, and as merciless with his enemies.

Sometimes they went without food for days because their pursuers were nearby, forcing them to take to the heather and live like wild animals until it was safe to risk moving on. More often than not the poor hovels they came upon as they moved further north had already been visited by MacLeod clansmen and there was no food to be found or, if it was, the villagers had already heard of what would happen to them and refused to part with it.

Men deserted them or were caught and killed, and their numbers dwindled from over twenty to less than a dozen. Duncan's decision for them to separate was made after three days of continual harassment by MacLeods, who seemed to come on them from all sides, no matter how many times they back-tracked or covered their trail.

Still weak from the beating she had received and unable to rest properly to restore her failing strength, Isabel was soon brought to the point of collapse. Simone and Duncan carried her between them until they, too, dropped exhausted on to the purple heather.

*   *   *

As soon as it was dark, the three of them began making their way towards Sandwood Loch and the ruined croft which lay above the bay. Isabel had reminded her brother of its existence and suggested it was a good place to wait while he contacted his friends and tried to find a boat to take them to France and safety. He had given her a strange look, but agreed, and she realised he was thinking of the night she and James had spent there. She remembered it too as she huddled in a corner trying to keep warm while Simone kept watch at the window. She closed her eyes and tried to sleep, but he was standing before her, ordering her to take off her wet clothes so that he could dry them and when she refused he had taken them off her himself.

Her cheeks burned at the remembrance of his impersonal touch—how different it had been when he had broken into her room at Asher Mor! That night she had slept with his plaid around her, warmed by the closeness of his body.

Without realising it she slept, and it was almost light when she opened her eyes. A heavy mist still hung over the water and it was unbearably cold. A fire would not be seen, she thought, but remembering Duncan's orders to the contrary she curbed the urge to go out and gather firewood. He would not return until that evening—a whole day without warmth or food, and she was in dire need of both. So too was Simone, still keeping a vigil at the window. She was almost to the door when the maid turned curiously.

'Where are you going?'

'We need food, Simone, perhaps I can find something—anything.'

'And walk straight into the arms of your brother's men.' Firmly Simone drew her back and made her sit down. 'I can steal a chicken even from under the fox's nose—I'll go. Promise me you won't leave here until I return.'

'I promise. Thank you, Simone—you are good to me.'

'And why not—it was you who first showed me how. Try to rest while I'm away.'

Isabel sat by the window watching the beach until Simone disappeared from sight. If she had not been so tired she would have insisted on going herself—after all, she did know the countryside, and then, again, perhaps Simone's upbringing in the back streets of the Beggars' Quarter gave her the advantage of stealth and cunning that was needed to avoid capture.

As the mists began to clear the sun came out for the first time in many days. Taking off her damp shoes and stockings, Isabel spread them on the floor in a patch of sunlight, relieved that she would at least have dry feet to continue the last part of her journey. If Duncan was successful in finding a friendly ship willing to take them they would all be in France, within a week.

She would go to the château, Isabel thought, not Versailles where she would have to face the gossip and wagging tongues all over again. The château—where Jean-Paul had dreamed of going to raise his horses. A shadow fell across her face and she looked up, ridding her mind of such morbid thoughts.

'Simone—you were quick——'

The words turned into a scream as the two clansmen standing in the doorway lunged towards her and dragged her to her feet. Her struggles were futile against their strength and she was dragged out on to the beach. Her senses reeled with the shock of what she saw. MacLeods were everywhere—searching the rocks along the cliffs—the ledges and the slopes behind the croft, and a few feet in front of her stood James—sword in one hand, the other shielding his eyes against the sun as he watched his men.

'Look what we've found, my lord,' one of her captors growled, pushing her forward but still retaining a painful grip on her arm.

James's face went blank with amazement as his eyes came to rest on the figure before him. The last time he had seen her, beside her father's grave, she had been shrouded from head to toe in black—sorrowing but beautiful—and her grief, even though he had ignored it, had touched him.

The young woman facing him now looked like a peasant's daughter or a fisherwoman. The blonde hair was loose about her shoulders, unkempt and clinging, still damp in places, to her pale face. She had grown thinner—what was left of the black mourning gown hung on her like a sack. Had it only been three weeks since she fled? It could have been three months. Only her eyes had not changed—they challenged him with all the defiance left in her weakened body.

'Are you alone?' he demanded harshly.

No kindness in his voice—nothing to give her any hope, Isabel thought, and was surprised that she had expected him to be any different. She had rehearsed this moment over and over in her mind, but now she was face to face with him nothing had changed.

'Yes.'

'Don't lie—Duncan wouldn't leave you alone so near De'n Ceo. Where is he? How many men are with you?' James's eyes grew dark with anger.

A stubborn look crossed Isabel's face and she stood silent.

'I'll make her tell you, my lord,' one of her guards snarled and struck her across the face with his clenched fist. It was a savage blow and she would have fallen had she not been securely held.

James was shocked to find his hand reaching instinctively for his sword. With an oath he withdrew it as if the hilt had been red-hot. Once he would have drawn his weapon to defend her against any man, but that time seemed an eternity ago and in another world.

'Leave her and join the others,' he snapped. He

motioned to the man who held Isabel. 'You—take her
back to the horses and guard her well.'

Isabel was dragged away so roughly that she almost
fell. She was sure James stood watching her, but she did
not look back. Let him waste his time searching, he
would not find Duncan; and if Simone returned while
the MacLeods were still at the croft she would hide and
go to warn him later.

Realising she was in no condition to give him a fight,
her guard relented and allowed her to walk on her own.
Isabel's eyes scanned the beach to her right—the tide
was going out and she could lose herself in the caves she
knew so well. If only—— She halted at the bottom of
the cliff path and looked upwards with a soft plea.

'May we rest—please? I can't climb up there yet.'

'Five minutes then—or you'll get me into trouble. No
tricks, mind.'

'Can I sit down?' Isabel pointed to a large rock
nearby, then her eyes flew over the man's shoulder and
she gave a startled gasp. 'Duncan!'

The trick worked. The man spun around, drawing
his sword. With all her strength, she threw herself
against his back and knocked him to the ground. He
lay still and it took her a full minute to realise he had
struck his head in falling and been knocked out. As
a shout went up heralding her action, she turned and
ran along the wet sand, fear lending wings to her bare
feet. At a curve in the cliffs she paused, breathless,
to look back. Men were above her, running to cut
her off, but only one man was behind her and it was
James!

The sight of him frightened her more than that of the
armed clansmen. Hampered by her long skirts as she
ran through the pools of water left by the receding tide
among the seaweed-covered rocks, she tripped and fell
heavily on to them. A searing pain went through her
shoulder as she pulled herself to her feet and she felt

something warm trickling down her back. She had cut herself, but there was no time to stop, James was almost upon her. Men were clambering down towards the beach only a few yards away as she ran on, and in a desperate attempt to avoid capture she headed towards the water. If she could swim around the point she could hide in the caves and they would never find her. Each gasping breath brought pain to her chest; she felt as if she was choking and her legs were as heavy as two wooden blocks.

The water was waist-high about her as James grabbed her arm and began to pull her back. Her struggles only succeeded in infuriating him to the extent where he seized her by the hair and pushed her under bodily. As she came back to the surface, coughing and gasping for precious breath, he waded back to the sand and threw her down. She lay there only half-conscious, listening to him issuing orders to his men, but unable to hear him closely. Her head felt as if it was about to burst. Weakly she rolled over on to her side and saw that where she had lain the sand was smeared with blood.

James saw it too, but she was too dazed to notice the panic which flashed into his eyes. Kneeling at her side, he ripped the material away from her shoulders. The cut was not a deep one, only superficial, but had bled quite profusely.

'It's only a scratch—you'll live,' he said tersely.

Isabel felt his fingers probing the damaged area and steeled herself not to flinch at his touch. She did not try to move away; what was the use? His men—all but one standing several feet away—were all going back to finish their search by the croft. If only she had the strength to run again, but she hadn't—she was finished—his prisoner. She winced as James went on with his examination and hoped he did not see it. He would expect weakness, but she would show him none.

She stiffened then as he ran his fingers down her back. He had seen the marks still visible from Malcolm's beating. Slowly she raised her head to look into his face. It was expressionless, his dark eyes unfathomable.

'Malcolm?' It was framed as a statement of fact rather than a question.

'If I say yes you will ask Malcolm, and he will deny it and you will, of course, believe him because he's proved me a liar in the past.'

'I'll ask him—when I deliver you to him,' James returned.

'You—you are taking me to him?'

Isabel drew back with an involuntary shudder. What was she still hoping for—James's conscience to trouble him? One look at his hard features told her that there was no chance of that.

'Why not?' James stood up and stared down at her pitilessly. 'And if you try to run again you'll have a few more bruises before you reach him. You may not know it but Malcolm isn't concerned how you reach him. He gave me free licence with you—so long as I returned you alive.'

His words robbed Isabel of all speech. Her shocked gaze searched desperately for an avenue of escape, but with James hovering over her and the guard beyond, there was none—and yet there was—just one. The sgian-dhu in James's stocking swam before her eyes and the next moment it was in her hand.

Whether or not she would have had the courage to use it on herself, which had been the mad thought which ran through her mind as she snatched it, she never had the chance to find out, for James knocked her back on to the sand and her wrist was seized in an agonising grip which made her cry out in pain. She stabbed down with the weapon before it was wrenched from her nerveless fingers, but it was not until the clansman hauled her to her feet that she saw the blood

welling down James's left arm and realised where the
blade had found a home.

'Take her back to the horses—tie her on,' came the
brutal order. 'If she gives you any trouble, knock her
out.'

They were almost as far as De'n Ceo; Isabel could just
see it jutting out on its tiny island below them. Another
hour and she would be face to face with Malcolm.
Would she live to see the end of the day? she wondered.
Her hands were tied in front of her, the ropes so tight
they cut into her skin, but she had not made a sound as
she was bound—nor as they bundled her roughly on to
a horse. James had given his orders and she knew his
men would carry them out. He rode in front of them all,
the sleeve of his jacket growing a darker red as the ride
continued.

The horses halted for a moment, then went on, and it
was a moment before her mind, so dazed with pain and
tiredness, realised that they had turned in the direction
of De'n Ceo. As they cantered along the causeway and
into the courtyard, James fell back to ride beside her.
Her questioning look was met with a blank stare. He
would tell her nothing until he was ready and she knew
it was useless to ask.

Bran MacKay came out to meet them. He scarcely
looked at Isabel being pulled unceremoniously from
her horse and was more concerned for his wounded
master, but James brushed aside his questions, ordering him to take charge of his prisoner.

She was led along a vaguely familiar corridor and
into a room filled with sunlight instead of the dark attic
she had been expecting. Her bonds were cut and she
was left alone. As the key turned in the lock behind
Bran MacKay she stood in the middle of the room that
had once belonged to James's mother—the very one
she had planned to use herself when she became his

wife. Isabel wept bitterly. He would never know how cruelly he had hurt her by imprisoning her here.

She slept the whole of that day and night and well into the morning of the following day. The sound of the door being unlocked stirred her into wakefulness. She expected James, come to gloat, but it was Bran Mac-Kay who stood to one side to allow a maid carrying a tray of food to enter. Isabel had not eaten in three days and she was ravenous. She cleared the plates regardless of the two silent onlookers, and afterwards began to feel human again. At least her stomach was taken care of, she thought, looking down at her dirty clothes.

Bran MacKay took the tray.

'The woman will look after you. If you wish for anything—ask her,' he said, and left them, relocking the door behind him.

A strange way to treat a prisoner, Isabel thought, watching the maid open one of the closets and begin to pull out some dresses.

'Would my lady care for a bath and a change of attire?'

Isabel wanted to refuse. When James came to exact his revenge she would have liked to have been as he had last seen her—a reminder of what he had helped to do to her—but the sight of the soft silken clothes, so clean and fresh, and the promise of a bath—— It was too much to refuse.

The maid was the only one to enter her rooms during the next three days, but Isabel knew Bran MacKay hovered outside the door whenever it was unlocked for any length of time.

The long days of solitude, although good for her health, almost drove her mad. She spent hours sitting by the window, watching the sea, or pacing through the rooms until her feet ached. Once she even tried hammering on the door, but of course no one came, and at

last she came to accept that she was to stay a prisoner—alone—until James decided otherwise. Once
she had accepted the fact, the loneliness grew easier to
bear—at least while she was here she was safe from
Malcolm.

Simone and Duncan would be worried out of their
wits by her disappearance. She prayed they would do
nothing reckless, such as trying to get near enough to
De'n Ceo to find out if she had been captured. Her heart
grew cold to think that they might go near Asher Mor.

For two more days the routine was unchanged. Her
needs were attended to by the stolid-faced maid who,
although competent, obviously had orders not to make
conversation, and each time after her visits the door
was locked. It was not until the afternoon of the fifth
day that Isabel realised anything had changed. She had
finished her meal and the tray had been removed. Out
of habit she sat and watched the maid open and close
the door and waited for the key to turn in the lock.
There was no sound and it was then she realised that
Bran MacKay had not been hovering in the doorway.
It was a trick, she thought. James wanted her to try and
escape just to have the pleasure of watching her dragged back—perhaps Malcolm and his men were waiting
in the corridor for her to walk straight into their arms.

Running to the windows she looked down into the
courtyard. It was deserted. With trembling hands she
eased the door open and looked out into the corridor—it, too, was empty. Without knowing why, she
closed it again and turned back into the room. When
the maid brought her evening meal Isabel was seated
on the low curving window seat in the sitting-room, her
head resting in her arms, and the presence of the other
woman was ignored.

She hardly ate any food, torn between the desire to
confront James and demand to know his intentions and
that of remaining where she was. Once she went outside

her apartments she had no knowledge of what she
might be confronted with.

Putting aside the tray she went into the bedroom and
stared at herself in the mirror. The velvet dress she wore
clung to her curvaceous body, still a trifle thin from the
weeks of privation, and there was still a bruise at the
corner of her mouth where the clansman had struck her;
but apart from that she thought she had come out of it all
remarkably well. At least James had given her the chance
of looking once again like herself and not a beggar-
woman. Why, she would never understand. The closet
full of clothes had belonged to his mother, yet he allowed
her to use them—to live in her apartments, to sleep in the
huge bed with its beautiful pale yellow silk sheets—the
bed she should have been sharing with him. That thought
had given her many restless hours, and prompted her
once again into believing her presence here was in some
way an act of revenge on his part.

Smoothing back her loose hair, she opened the bedroom door and stepped purposefully outside. She
passed a servant as she reached the end of the corridor,
but was not challenged. As she descended the stairs
Bran MacKay came out of one of the downstairs rooms
and stood watching her. Isabel measured the distance
to the main doors, but knew he could get there before
her if she tried to run. She came down to face him,
proud, challenging.

'I want to see your master.'

'I advise against it—he is not in a good mood
tonight, my lady.'

How polite he was! Isabel could not hide her surprise, and a faint smile touched the steward's face.

'My master has allowed you the run of the house so
long as you do not attempt to leave.'

'And if I do?' Her tawny eyes sparkled defiance.

'Then I will stop you,' Bran returned, his tone hardening slightly, and she knew he would.

'Why was the door left unlocked?'

'Those were my instructions.'

Isabel looked past him to the closed doors through which he had just come and, ignoring his warning look, she stepped past him and went in. Instead of trying to stop her, he merely closed the doors behind her, leaving her alone in the ill-lit room—alone except for the figure sprawled in a chair before a blazing fire.

It was not a comfortably furnished room—the furniture was sparse, the walls covered with weapons instead of tapestries, the floor uncovered, but it was James's favourite room, the one where he could always be alone. All the servants knew better than to disturb him while he lingered with his memories of the past in this one place he had shared in common with his father.

He was stretching out for the bottle of whisky on the table beside him when he became aware of the figure approaching. Deliberately he refilled his glass and sat back before looking up. Isabel came to an abrupt halt a few feet away, hoping she masked the sudden apprehension she felt at his appearance. His face had several days' growth of beard on it and his normally alert dark eyes were lined with weariness—or was it too much liquor? His ruffled shirt was open almost to the waist, but he made no attempt to tidy his appearance at her arrival. He was half drunk, she thought. The bandage on his arm was spotted with fresh blood and had not been changed.

'I was expecting you.' James swallowed his drink and instantly refilled the glass.

'Is that why my door was left unlocked?'

'I wanted to see what you would do. I knew you would come eventually, but you're wasting your time—you have nothing of interest left to give me in return for your freedom.'

Isabel blanched at his scornful words. So that was what he expected—and believing what he did about her, it was not so unnatural—but how it hurt! Was there nothing left between them?

'Why have you brought me to De'n Ceo?' Isabel demanded.

James raised his head and looked at her fully for the first time, and a tight knot formed in his stomach at the sight of her lovely face. If only he had turned her over to Malcolm as soon as he had captured her; but he had wanted her to suffer as he had, to remember her promises and regret them—to come to him and beg for her freedom. The desire for revenge had obliterated everything else in his mind, and yet in the end it was all meaningless. She would never beg, and if she had he would have wanted to kill her.

'Why?' He deliberated on the question for a long moment, deliberately prolonging her agony. 'What's wrong? Are the bridal apartments not comfortable?'

'I knew it. You want to torture me with the plans we made, don't you? Watch me and gloat, and hope I'll crawl to you. How long am I to be kept here?'

'For as long as I choose.'

Or until I weaken, James mused silently. Already his body ached with the longing to possess her. All he had to do was reach out and take her. She stepped back in alarm as he sprang to his feet and the glass he had been holding was flung on to the hearth where it shattered into a hundred pieces. He was drunk, but in control of his actions, Isabel realised, and remembering how his temper had been inflamed with whisky the day Jean-Paul had been killed, she began to wonder if this was his way of finding the courage to kill her. He had threatened it——

'Am I to be turned over to Malcolm?'

'As far as he's concerned you are still at large. If you wish I can send for him—the choice is yours.' James moved closer, his burning gaze centred on her pale face.

'No——' Isabel bit her lip, wishing she had not answered so quickly.

'Then go back to your rooms and don't leave them again.'

He was so close to her she could smell the whisky on his breath, but she did not move—the look in his eyes held her rooted to the spot. The longing was still there, so was the hatred and the bitterness——

'In God's name, what do you want from me?' Isabel cried.

James's hands fastened over her shoulders, biting into the bare skin just above the line of her gown. She could feel the restrained emotion fighting to be unleashed and felt faint with the longing for him to hold her—even make love to her. What did it matter so long as he kept her with him?

'What I want I'll take in my own good time and on my terms, Madame la Marquise. On my terms.'

'Do you mean to keep me here as your plaything?' Isabel's voice was hardly audible.

James's face took on a terrible expression—his hands loosened their grasp, only to move purposefully around her slim throat and tighten slowly.

'Do you want to know why I brought you here?' he snarled. 'To kill you—damn it—to end your worthless life as you ended mine, but more slowly—like this.'

His fingers increased their pressure until his face swam before Isabel's tortured vision. Her hands groped for his shirt and clutched at it desperately as her senses reeled.

'James!'

The ruthless pressure ceased as if he had only just become aware of his actions. Isabel tottered backwards, clutching her bruised throat, fighting against the faintness which engulfed her. She felt the door against her back and wrenched it open in relief. James did not even look up as she ran upstairs.

CHAPTER
TEN

EARLY the following morning James rode away from De'n Ceo, accompanied by Bran MacKay. Isabel watched them go from her window, then returned to bed. He had gone to fetch her brother; there was nothing left to do but wait.

When the horses were slowed to a walking pace the steward ventured to ask of the silent man at his side.

'Are we going to Asher Mor, my lord?'

'I am. You will stay out of sight of the house and wait for me. If I don't appear by dusk you will go back to De'n Ceo and get the woman to safety. Do I make myself clear?' James looked at his companion and laughed at the incredulity on his face. 'No, I'm not mad, Bran—just in full possession of my sanity again. While Malcolm's hatred of his sister exists her life will always be in danger, and I don't propose that my wife should live in fear for the rest of her life.'

How easy it was to talk this way now he had taken the all-important decision to see Malcolm, he mused. He would try to talk to him first, but if that proved useless he would have to kill him. He did not care which way the matter was settled so long as he could return to Isabel and tell her she was no longer in danger from her brother and himself. He would beg her forgiveness, on his knees if necessary. God! What did France matter? Whatever indiscretions she had committed she had been driven to them by Malcolm's fanatical jealousy, and the years spent with the old man to whom she had been sacrificed.

The thought of those years made James's blood boil,

but he would make them up to her. She suspected the worst in his actions, not knowing how deeply he had been affected by her in his arms—and she had watched them leave, he had glimpsed her in the window as he mounted.

Bran MacKay stared into his master's determined face. He was only a few years older than James, but he had served him long and faithfully and never questioned any orders. They often hunted together and since the death of the mistress of De'n Ceo he had been treated more as a friend, yet he had never learned to understand James's moods—or accept that he would never marry, as James so vehemently declared every time the subject arose.

Secretly he had been pleased when Isabel invaded his solitary existence. She had the grace and charm needed to make De'n Ceo a home again and she would give James bonny children to make the old place ring with happy laughter once more.

Bran was not listening to him. His interest suddenly centred on the two figures running through the heather in front of them.

'Women from the village,' Bran muttered, but James reined in his horse with an abrupt oath.

'One of them is Mary MacLeod,' he cried and leapt from the saddle. He reached Mary's side just as her strength failed her and she fell half fainting into his arms. As he lowered her to the ground the second woman leapt on to his back, trying to pull him away and screaming at him in a language he could not understand but knew to be Isabel's second tongue—French.

Spinning round, he slapped Simone to the ground, and Bran's foot against her throat, plus the sight of his sword menacing her, momentarily stilled her.

'Where is my mistress? What have you done to her, you heathen devil?'

'She is safe—which is more than you will be if you

don't keep a civil tongue in your head,' James snapped, and bent over Mary MacLeod, his face hardening at the sight of her distraught features. She was still fighting for breath and he wondered where her horse had got to. As if she read his thoughts Mary said jerkily:

'I am on foot. It was—was the only way I could get out of the house without Malcolm growing suspicious.'

'Where were you going?'

'To see you—to—to——' She broke off and buried her face in her hands.

'To feed you more of her lies,' Simone cried out behind them and was abruptly silenced by the increased pressure of Bran's foot across her throat.

'Let her go,' James ordered. 'I want the answers to some questions, and one way or the other I intend to have them.'

'Madame—*mignonne*—oh, you are safe! I didn't believe him.'

Isabel had never seen Simone cry before, not even when Jean-Paul had been killed, but now, in the courtyard at De'n Ceo, she held the girl in her arms and wept.

'*Mon Dieu*, I imagined such terrible things. Are you sure he hasn't harmed you—you are so pale. He hasn't——'

'Made love to me?' Isabel finished the sentence for her with a faint smile. 'Not even that. I almost wish he had. There is such hurt in him, Simone—so much pent-up emotion. It would have been better had he poured it out on me. I am the one to blame, after all.'

'No—she is the one to blame.' Simone pointed a shaking finger at Mary MacLeod, whom Bran was helping to dismount. Isabel's face registered instant displeasure at the sight of the person who had so unfairly maligned her.

'What is she doing here?'

'She was on her way here—troubled by her conscience and anxious to unload it on to someone else. I saw her leave Asher Mor and followed, and I would have killed her if I had not been prevented,' Simone declared with a fierce scowl. 'She deserves to die for what she did to Jean-Paul and you.'

Isabel looked about her, suddenly realising the absence of James.

'Where is James?' When Simone did not answer, she turned to Bran. 'Where did your master go?'

'To Asher Mor.' It was Mary who answered, her voice almost inaudible. She looked terrible and was clinging heavily to the steward's arm. He cast an anxious look at Isabel.

'Help me to get her inside, my lady, she's ill. And you were told to find Duncan MacLeod,' he said to Simone, who hovered by their side as they helped Mary into the house. 'Bring him here as quickly as possible.'

Simone hesitated, loath to leave her mistress again so soon, but the knowledge that Isabel would never forgive her if she allowed anything to happen to her precious James prompted her into action. While Isabel bent over Mary MacLeod, she slipped out unnoticed.

'She is with child,' Bran muttered.

'That explains much. She is very weak—is there somewhere she could rest for a while?'

'I'll have one of the upstairs rooms prepared.'

'Stay with me.' Mary caught one of Isabel's hands as she tried to rise. 'Forgive me! Please!'

'When love controls our lives we do strange things. I bear you no ill will—not now I understand,' Isabel said gently, and it was the truth. Duncan was vindicated and James—— She rose to her feet so abruptly that Mary's eyes grew wide with alarm.

'What is it?'

'James! You said he went to Asher Mor.'

'To kill Malcolm. He sent for Duncan to come here

and protect you should he not return. How long have you been here?'

'How long?' Isabel repeated slowly. It seemed an eternity. 'Nearly a week—most of the time locked upstairs.'

'I brought you to this with my lies. I never intended James to turn against you so violently—to bring you here and——'

'And nothing, Mary. Whatever his reasons, I have been treated well.'

'How he must love you!'

'He hates me.'

'That isn't true. If he did he would have turned you over to Malcolm instead of bringing you here. You are under his protection at De'n Ceo; not even Malcolm would risk coming to fetch you, and you tell me he hasn't touched you. Don't you understand what that means? He never intended to give you up! He has never stopped loving you. Where are you going?' Her voice rose anxiously as Isabel turned towards the door.

'You know where.'

'But Malcolm will kill you if he still lives.'

'If he is still alive, then James is dead and so am I. I would prefer to die too, rather than live without him.'

Bran came running downstairs, brought by Mary's frantic cries, but by the time he reached the door Isabel had already taken a horse and was out of sight.

What Isabel had said to Mary had been the truth. Without James she was as good as dead. She knew now that even if Duncan had managed to take her to France she would have returned, with or without him. She was bound to James by a love far stronger than any chains—it demanded she gave everything and if that included her life, she was willing.

The guards at the main gates stared in amazement at

the woman who galloped past them and then called an urgent warning to other MacLeods near by. Isabel shook off the hands which reached up to pull her from her saddle with such disdain they drew back and made no further move to touch her.

'Take me to my brother,' she ordered, and was led into the house, watched by silent clansmen who looked at each other in puzzlement and wondered at her sudden appearance. Each and every one of them knew what would happen to her. For weeks they had scoured the hills searching relentlessly to find Duncan's band, sworn at continuously by the new laird as their prey constantly eluded them and marvelled at the luck which kept them at large.

Malcolm came out of the library and stared at her as if she was an apparition, then he began to chuckle. It was an unpleasant sound which sent a shiver down Isabel's back. How many times as a child had she heard the same hateful sound?

'So you came to find him? Isabel, you never cease to amaze me. Such concern—or are you really in love with James after all?'

'Where is he?' She looked around frantically, seeking some sign to tell her James was still alive.

'Enjoying my hospitality. He was seen talking to Mary less than two hours ago and so he was expected. I never expected the fool to come alone. She told him everything, I suppose?'

'Everything, and now she's safely at De'n Ceo where you can't touch her.'

Malcolm's eyes wandered slowly over her appearance, his face breaking into a sardonic smile.

'As you have been by the look of you—that dress certainly didn't come from any villager. So James has been keeping you at De'n Ceo—how easy for you both. He always was too soft-hearted. I was hoping he'd kill you and save me the trouble.'

'Where is he?' Isabel's self-control snapped and she would have thrown herself at him had she not been seized by one of the MacLeods standing watchfully around them.

'Escort my sister to James MacLeod,' Malcolm said with a laugh.

Isabel was not taken to the dungeons below the house, which was where she had imagined James to be imprisoned, but down the narrow twisting steps which led to the caves. Her steps faltered as the door leading down to them was reached and she heard her brother chuckling in the shadows near by, knowing the fearful memories this place held for her. She slipped and almost fell on the steps, still wet from the water which had covered it at high tide, was hauled roughly to her feet again and pushed on into the very cave where Jean-Paul had held Andrew Beaton a prisoner.

She knew the choice was a deliberate attempt on Malcolm's part to frighten her, perhaps make her beg for her life. She was frightened—terrified—as she was seized bodily and carried towards the yawning chasm at the far end. Her screams echoed around the cavern and she called James's name just once before the ground rushed up to meet her and knocked the breath from her body. She lay face down on the wet sand which had broken her fall, bruised and dazed until something touched her cheek and she rolled over with a startled cry.

'Isabel!' James's voice came out of the darkness—startled—disbelieving, but all she could see of him was a vague outline framed against the flickering light of the torches held by the clansmen some twenty feet above. She grasped at the hands which touched her and pulled herself up into his arms.

'James! I was so frightened. Are you hurt?' Not waiting for an answer, she ran anxious fingers over his face and along his forehead and down his arms and felt blood on his sleeve. His wound had opened again. If he had been unable to defend himself it was her fault.

'James—oh, my love, why did you come alone?'

'And you? How are you here?' James's voice was noticeably unsteady and she smiled in the darkness, sensing the indecision raging in him.

'I followed you. To live or die at your side—where I belong. Oh, why won't you believe I love you?'

James's mouth on hers was more eloquent than any words, and all mistrust melted away in that single moment.

'I believe you. Last night when I held you I knew I still loved you—nothing could ever change the way I feel. I have no excuses for the way I've acted—I think I must love you too much. Forgive me——'

'Hush, don't reprove yourself——' Isabel tilted her face to his again and surrendered to the wild kisses pressed on her mouth. Her body trembled and she strained closer to his, desperately seeking to shut out the hopelessness of their situation.

'I love you,' James whispered tenderly and repeated it between each kiss, allowing himself to be consumed by the passions he had denied for so long. A long, low laugh from above brought him back to his senses and he drew back, staring up into Malcolm's distorted features. The black-hearted swine was enjoying every moment, he thought disgustedly. Groping for Isabel's hand, he drew her up against him, whispering:

'How well do you know these caves? Is there a way out of here?'

'Not from where we are at this moment,' Isabel answered, and heard him swear under his breath. She stared into the darkness towards the hole, no more than a foot across, through which the water would come when the tide turned. They could not squeeze through nor climb up the face of the rock to safety, and the ledge where Andrew Beaton had been left to deliberate his conscience was at fingertip height. That, too, would be submerged eventually. 'He means to leave us here to drown.'

James groaned inwardly at his own helplessness. If only he had a weapon—— Suddenly he leapt to his feet, appealing to the silent watcher above.

'Let her go—she's your sister. For the love of God, man, let her live.'

'You disappoint me, James—from you I expected anger, not this,' Malcolm mocked. He could hardly see James's face, but it gave him great satisfaction to hear the entreaty in his voice and to think of his clever sister huddling in the darkness, waiting for the water to start creeping around her legs. She would be remembering the last time, he thought with malicious amusement. She had always hated the dark. He would wait an hour or so and then come back—by then she might have reached the begging stage—and how he wanted to hear her beg. It was a pity Duncan could not be down there too—but that would come later.

'Leave a torch for the two love-birds,' he instructed the waiting MacLeods, and motioned them to leave. Leaning over the edge he stared down at the shadowy figure of James. 'You have two or three hours. I'd make the most of them if I were you.'

James's vehement curses followed him out of the cave. He leaned against the hard rock, beating at it with his clenched fists until Isabel came to his side and wrapped her arms around him and laid her head against his shoulders, saying quietly, calmly:

'Come and rest, James—you will need your strength. There is nothing we can do.'

'Nothing?' His voice was hollow with despair. 'We have so much to live for.'

'Don't—at least we are together. Come and sit down—I want to talk to you. It's easy here in the darkness—I can say all the things I've never had the courage to before.'

'It doesn't matter now, Isabel, leave it.' His voice became almost angry at her acceptance of the situation. 'Nothing matters now, does it?'

'Don't be angry with me, James—listen, please. Once before when I wanted to tell you about France, you said it could wait until after we were married. It can't wait any longer, and it's important that you know everything about me—about my scandalous behaviour. Hold me.'

He took her in his arms in silence and she gained courage from his nearness. It was even possible not to think of that cold water——

'It all began, of course, with Malcolm using me as payment for his gambling debts, and after that Julian held me responsible for us not having a child. The knowledge that he could never have a precious son and heir drove him to the point of insanity. It was an obsession, you know—one which ruled our lives until the day he died. I tried to run away once, after he had told me he must have a son—by any means. He sent men after me, hired from the gutter by the promise of gold. I never ran away again——'

She shivered and James gently stroked her hair, waiting for her to regain her composure. Something Simone had once said drifted into his mind. 'Madame tried to escape after eight months of marriage. The inhuman monster hired two men—scum—to go after her. You should have seen how they brought her back —tied to the pommel of her horse like a runaway servant.'

'I hope Simone is safe. I don't think I would have survived for so long without her,' Isabel murmured.

'How did she and her brother come to be with you?' James asked. That question had always intrigued him.

'They owned a tavern near the Pont-Neuf when I first met them. Julian and I had been to the theatre, but on the way home he decided he was too tired to go to supper and left me with friends. I ended up in the company of a young man intent on seducing me. Julian surrounded me with young men, hoping I would see a prospective lover in one of them and have an *affaire*. More than one if it meant I gave him a son.

'Why Simone and Jean-Paul befriended me that night I'll never know. He hated the aristocracy, and for months after he came into my service I was in fear he would steal everything he could lay his hands on. Simone was wonderful and gradually I came to realise they were sincere in their efforts to help me. No matter what their intentions in the beginning, they grew to be the only two people I could trust. They hated Julian and he feared Jean-Paul, whom he knew would protect me at all costs.'

'I was a blind fool to misinterpret your relationship,' James said.

'You saw more than I,' Isabel's voice was full of sadness. 'I had to fall in love with you before I realised how deeply Jean-Paul felt. He gave me so much, and in return I hurt him terribly. Even his murderer goes unpunished. Living with Julian was not unlike living with Malcolm, do you know that? Both of them enjoyed seeing others suffer—inflicting punishment perhaps gave greater pleasure. When Julian realised I would not take a lover, willingly or by threat, he devised other means to beget an heir. I had been staying at the château while he remained at Versailles, ill he said. When I came back I expected to be plagued with the usual men and parties, but instead he allowed me to lead a normal life. A doctor confirmed that he was ill and for the first time in nearly four years I was free of him.

'And that was when I met the Comte du Ruyon. He was older—quieter than the circle of people I had been forced to mix with—polite and an excellent conversationalist, but totally uninterested in the Marquise de Riché. You don't know how relieved I was to have a friend—after the continual flow of men whose only thoughts were to get me into bed.'

'Did you love him?' James hated himself for asking the question. Isabel's hair brushed his cheek as she turned, and her lips lightly touched his. 'I'm sorry—but the thought of anyone else holding you——'

'Julian held me, James—I was his wife and he had the right, but not once in all those times did he ever make me feel as I do now, just lying here in your arms. In a few moments you have taught me more about love—and about myself—than he ever could. I was nothing to him—my body an object he owned, to be used and abused when it suited him. Even if you had taken me at De'n Ceo I could not have hated you— I find it difficult to hate. I fear Malcolm. Julian I pitied, and I think there was a little hatred, too, for all those years of humiliation, but the only man I really hated was de Ruyon. I thought he was my friend and he betrayed me. It was impossible not to see a lot of each other at court, but our friendship, or what I considered to be friendship, developed slowly. Whenever we dined together, it was never alone and his manners were above reproach. He was clever—and completely heartless. Gradually I came to enjoy his company, knowing I had nothing to fear while with him.

'Julian knew he sometimes escorted me and made the usual crude suggestions, which I ignored. The night Julian died I had been to a *bal masqué* with de Ruyon, and it was late when he returned me to the house. Jean-Paul and Simone had gone back to see old friends at the tavern, and he chose the one night I was alone to follow me into the house and try to make love to me.

'Julian had hired him to get to know me. I later learned he was an adventurer who had fled to Italy from Paris after a rather sordid scandal with a woman. At first I thought he had had too much to drink, but he laughed at that while we struggled together and told me he had been paid handsomely to seduce me. He would have succeeded too, if Julian hadn't chosen that moment to come out of his room. He wanted to watch, James—it gave him pleasure to hear me beg, to see me fight against a man I had no chance of defeating.

'His pleasure killed him. He was urging de Ruyon on when his heart failed and he collapsed at the top of the stairs. De Ruyon panicked and ran, leaving me alone with Julian, but there was nothing I could do, he was quite dead. His death released me from a tormentuous existence, but straight away I was plunged into another.

'De Ruyon began rumours that he was my lover—to cover himself in case I brought charges of assault, I suppose. Julian had often allowed people to believe I was unfaithful and the story was believed. He told everyone how he had been at the house the night my husband had died—that Julian must have been dying in his bed while he made love to me.'

'My God!' James ejaculated. It was the same rumour that Malcolm had related to him and he—fool that he was—had believed it.

'You can hardly blame people for believing it, James—I was so much younger than Julian, and the men he befriended were well paid to keep silent. At first I wanted to leave—then, despite the scandal I was invited back to court after the mourning period was over. The shallowness of it all made me want to stay and fight. I had position and money of my own. I played men at their own game and Jean-Paul was my protection. It was heartless, but it was my way of paying them back. It did little to enhance my already colourful reputation, I'm afraid.'

'A pity I could not have met this de Ruyon,' James said harshly.

'Jean-Paul called him out over a trifling incident and killed him. It was quite deliberate, but he made sure I knew nothing about it until it was all over. Can you understand now why I called him my true friend?'

'Do you realise that if I had known all this in the beginning we might not be here?'

'Would you have admitted you loved me knowing I came back to help Duncan——' She broke off, sudden excitement rising inside her. 'Simone has gone to fetch him! He will come after me, James! We have a chance.'

'Of course—I'd forgotten.' James drew her head down on to his shoulder. 'Now you must save your strength. Try to sleep.'

Within minutes her soft regular breathing told him she was asleep and he breathed a sigh of relief, grateful she had not been aware that the water was already beginning to seep back into the cave. He had been aware of it for some while.

Carefully, so as not to awaken her, he carried her to the far side where the sand was still dry and covered her with his coat, then he left her to feel his way along the slippery rock face for some uneven piece which might give him a foothold and the chance of a way out for them both. But there was nothing. After what seemed hours of trying, he managed with a supreme effort to haul himself up on to the ledge, but his strength was gone and his raw-skinned hands still could not reach their objective.

He was weak from loss of blood, and the continuous strain on his arm had caused the wound to begin bleed-

ing again. He tried one desperate lunge upwards, but
his numb fingers clawed hopelessly against solid rock
and threw him off balance—down once again on to the
sand—sand that was now completely covered with
water.

Simone caught Duncan's arm with a cry of alarm at the
sight which met their eyes as they climbed down to the
beach.

'Look! The water has almost half covered the cave
entrance. How can we get in?'

'We swim,' came the determined reply. 'You don't
have to.'

'Yes I do, my mistress is in that devil's house,'
Simone muttered fiercely.

'She is also my sister,' Duncan reminded her.
'Come—we don't have much time if we are to reach the
door before the caves are flooded.'

'Do you think Mary MacLeod will keep her word
and open the door?' Simone had to run to keep up with
his long strides. They were not alone—he had brought
half a dozen MacLeods with him—three who had
followed him from the beginning, and three of James's
men. The remainder, under Bran, had ridden to Asher
Mor openly seeking James's whereabouts. Duncan
hoped the diversion would allow them to get inside
unseen and effect a rescue of the prisoners before they
could be harmed. With each step he prayed that Isabel
was not already dead. Could he trust Mary? He
shrugged his shoulders.

'We will see,' he said grimly. 'How well can you
swim?'

'Like a fish.'

'I hope so.' Motioning the men to follow, he waded
out into the water and began to swim strongly towards
the half-submerged cave-mouth a hundred yards away.
Without hesitation Simone plunged after him.

A strong current swept them in the right direction, out of strong sunlight into shadowy caverns where the waves broke against the solid rock and bounced back over them, almost drowning them with spray.

The main tunnel was not yet flooded—Duncan stopped swimming as the steps loomed up in front of him and found that the water was only waist high. He stared thoughtfully at the wall torches burning over his head. It meant someone had been down here recently. The others joined him, shaking the water from their hair and eyes. Simone stood at his side, one hand on the knife pushed into the waistband of her skirt. She had come not only for Isabel, Duncan knew, but seeking vengeance for the death of her brother. If she got to Malcolm first she would kill him.

'Someone has been here,' he motioned to the torches. 'The woman, perhaps.'

Duncan climbed the steps and tried the door. It yielded to his touch and opened to reveal the figure of Mary MacLeod crouching back against the wall.

'You came—I thought——'

'Where is Isabel?' Catching her arm he dragged her forward into the light. 'If you've lied and this is a trap——' He left the sentence unfinished meaningly.

'She must be in the dungeons—James, too—there is no sign of them upstairs. I've looked everywhere. I was still searching when James's men arrived and I came down here to find you.'

'They could be in one of a dozen places,' Duncan answered grimly. 'We'll just have to search them all.'

'Quiet—I think I can hear someone coming! I must close the door——'

Simone, who had slipped past Duncan, melted back into the shadows as Mary closed the door on him and began to lift the heavy wooden bars into place across it. She watched the man who came down the narrow passageway and her eyes blazed as one of the torches illuminated Malcolm's face, twisted into a grotesque mask of hate as he saw his wife and instantly realised what she was attempting to do. Above him James's men were being held at bay, but for how long he did not know, but it would be sufficient time for him to kill his sister and James MacLeod should the water not have already done so.

Simone watched and waited, the knife in her hand ready to strike. Absorbed in her task, Mary heard nothing—saw nothing—she died with Malcolm's sword blade through her heart and made no sound.

'You treacherous bitch.' He moved her roughly away from the door with his foot and then, with a smile, bent to pick up the last wooden post and replace it. 'All three of you together—it's fitting you die with one who has protected you so well, brother.'

He heard the soft footfall but turned too late and, unlike Mary, he saw the face of the person behind him—looked for an instant into the face which blazed with triumph and for a moment had a glimpse of himself. Then he toppled forward into the dirt and lay still.

'What the devil?' Duncan looked at her then at the two inert bodies. 'Mary——'

'He did it. He was going to leave you to drown, so I killed him. Duncan—he said something about you all dying together. Could it be they are somewhere down here—in this awful place?'

'Why not—he tried it once before. My God, the place is almost flooded.' Duncan flung himself back into the water, calling for the others to follow him. 'Search everywhere—they have to be here. We must find them—hurry, damn you—hurry——'

What followed was like a nightmare. The water rising higher with each passing minute—men flailing through the water—searching—calling—climbing and slipping over rocks and crevasses—calling—calling——

James, barely half conscious, heard the shouts echoing through the caves and for a time thought it was only his wild imagination. He had pushed Isabel up on to the ledge and had somehow managed to drag himself up after her, but the water had climbed too, bringing with it cold and agonising cramps which several times had rendered Isabel near to fainting. She was a dead weight in his arms, hovering between consciousness and unconsciousness, her face against his shoulder wet with spray and lost of all colour. Twice she had slipped beneath the water and he had pulled her back, but even he was beginning to have difficulty in keeping both of them afloat against the force of the tide. Soon he would be swept from the ledge, and then they would both be drowned.

This was how Simone found them, and her frantic cries brought Duncan and the rest of the men quickly to her side.

'Take her—take Isabel first.' James pushed her up towards the eager hands reaching down and promptly fainted. It was Duncan who dived to bring him to safety and when his senses returned James found himself lying in the passageway, his rescuer bending over him. A few feet away Isabel was cradled in Simone's arms; her eyes were still closed, and he started up fearfully.

'She's still alive—thanks to you.' Duncan found the words were not so hard. Once he and James had been friends. They looked at each other for a long moment and saw in each other's eyes that it would be so again in time. 'Your steward and men are in control of the house.'

'No,' James said with a deep breath, 'You are in control. Asher Mor belongs to you.'

'And Isabel to you. It seems I have found her again only to lose her.'

He watched James bend over his sister and lift her into his arms, saw the way she locked her arms about his neck and clung to him, oblivious to everyone but him.

'James, are we free? How did we get out of the caves?'

'Hush, little one, rest now.' James kissed her wet cheeks as he carried her out into the Great Hall. Simone began to follow, but Duncan caught her arm with a slow smile and drew her back into the circle of his arms.

'This is one time she has no need of either of us,' he murmured.

Isabel stirred in James's grasp and her arms tightened around his neck.

'Take me away from here,' she whispered. She had not seen Mary nor been told of Malcolm's death, and seeing the MacLeods in the hall she feared for their safety.

'Not yet, my love, it's best you remain here for the moment. Safer for you,' he added softly, and his dark eyes teased her as he bent to kiss her soft mouth.